The play of the game begins. . . .

She drove away without looking back at him. Her shock propelled her through the gathering parade crowds as if the Ford were a tank: people scattered, raised fists at her. She didn't care. In each face she saw someone watching her from the Game Committee.

Was all of Mexico part of the thing? Where did it stop—it was like the Aztec image of the serpent swallowing its own tail: The whole country fed on itself, devoured itself, according to the whims of some invisible men in some unknown place, like the old gods who had demanded human sacrifice. And now was it Luis's turn, her turn?

The 16th of September Game

Robert Houston

BALLANTINE BOOKS • NEW YORK

Library of Congress Catalog Card Number: 84-91021

ISBN 0-345-31785-8

Printed in Canada

First Edition: March 1985

For Granny, Hazel, Anita, Dannie, Martha.
With lasting love.

The author would like to thank Jorge Vega,
who first told him about the sixteenth of
September game.

The desert light *feels* red . . .

ROBERT PACK

One

THEY HAD EATEN THE PEACOCKS, GUADALUPE told her, horrified, half-moons of sweat spreading under the arms of the gray housekeeper's uniform that Kathleen had always thought made her look like a church bell. Eaten the peacocks, drained the water from the swimming pool to wash their clothes—such as they were—and ripped the tin roof off *el señor*'s

Cessna hangar to build their shacks. And they were living in every room out there in the country house, probably a dozen peasants to each broom closet, if you could call that living, and no doubt cooking their tortillas over fires made from all that wonderful furniture *el señor*'s grandfather had sent to Spain for. It was the end of the world, Guadalupe said, throwing her arms out to call all the white, unmoved furniture of the huge living room as her witness. It was Armageddon.

Kathleen tuned her out. It would have seemed strange to her once that a housekeeper could care more about the family property than the "mistress," the señora herself. But after a dozen years in Mexico, such righteously democratic New England nonsense had been plucked out of her like the memory of the smell of spruces. Yet still . . . still, Kathleen knew she should care more than she did: those lands that were being invaded by all those hungry peasants weren't just *el señor*'s, weren't just Jorge's alone. She was Jorge's wife. Even in Mexico that meant that the lands, the property, were hers, too.

Guadalupe's family could lose the jobs they'd had for God only knew how many generations, yes. But how about herself, how about Kathleen Zaragoza de Ballance and her family? How about her two older sons' schooling back in New England, then college for them? How about the special therapy Luis, her youngest son, would need up in Tucson so that he could talk to her, even if he could never hear her answer him? How about all that bravado that had

3

sustained her when she'd called her parents and announced she was going to marry a Mexican landowner in a town they'd never heard of two hundred miles below the border? Dear God, college in Arizona had been foreign enough to them. What would she do now if she and Jorge did lose the land—show up on the front porch of that sagging white house in the Green Mountains with her penniless husband and her children and say, Here we are, here's the smarter-than-you daughter who knew her own mind so wonderfully. Take us in, the whole brood.

"Whose people are at the country house?" she asked Guadalupe.

Guadalupe, round as a pomegranate and with a face forever worried, had always seemed to Kathleen somehow off balance, as if she were teetering on the edge of a cliff. She swayed a little now and flipped up her palms in a Mexican shrug, like a woman getting ready to catch a medicine ball. "Who knows, señora? *Quién sabe?* They say that communist woman tells them all what to do."

"Alicia Dura? What do you know about 'communists,' Lupe?" She checked herself. That was the kind of talk that always got her into trouble at the Landowners Club. "What about Jorge's men? Didn't they fight?"

"Oh, señora! How could they fight? Señor Jorge's off in Mexico City, nobody knows whose side the government is on, nobody knows how many peasants are out there, nobody knows if they've got guns. . . ."

Of course, Kathleen thought. *Quién sabe?* Who

4

knows? Who knows anything for certain? This was Mexico. If she lived here another fifty years, she'd never get used to trying to get by in a country that lived by the rumor, a country where you never knew anything for certain from one day to the next. Everybody in Mexico seemed always to be trying to leap from one lifeboat to another in a fog—and there was never a shore in sight anywhere.

She had a quick moment of fear. Where was her lifeboat? Two hundred miles away at an imaginary line in the Sonoran desert called a border? Two thousand miles away in a green, cedar-shingled town in Vermont that might as well be on the moon? A thousand miles away in a hotel room in Mexico City where Jorge and a committee were trying to bribe, plead, demand—anything—to get the government to send troops, to negotiate, to tell him there *would* be a lifeboat?

In six hours, she could be at the border. She could put Luis in the car now and simply leave, be in Nogales before dark. Federico and Jaime were safe in school in Vermont—she could call her parents and tell them to pick the boys up and meet her in Burlington by tomorrow.

Like hell she would. She'd tolerated the suffocatingly proper, hypocritical world of these Mexican upper classes a dozen years for the sake of Jorge and for the children as they came along. No matter how much she might feel for those hungry people squatting out there on the land, no matter how little she might really care what happened to Jorge's hangar and the antique furniture and those foul-tempered peacocks who had strutted all over the lawn, no matter how lonely she'd been these dozen years and would probably continue to be if she stayed here—no matter any of that, this life was the only one she had now.

She crossed the echoing tiles of the living room to the phone and dialed Jorge's hotel. New Englanders were supposed to be tough, weren't they? All right. Be tough, Kathleen.

"Who told you about the country house?" she asked Guadalupe while Teléfonos Mexicanos fed her its obligatory hisses and clicks through the long distance lines.

"Ramón, señora. He's outside in the truck."

"Fine foreman! The first thing he does is run here and hide."

Guadalupe pursed her lips and scowled eloquently. The fact that Ramón was her husband notwithstanding, he was the best, most loyal foreman in the Yaqui Valley and they both knew it.

"Oh, damn, Lupe, I'm not interested in being fair right now." Ashamed, she turned her back on Guadalupe. "The last place he should be hanging around is here. Tell him to keep moving, keep finding out whatever he can. I'm calling Señor Jorge."

She heard Guadalupe's plastic soles slap away across the tiles as the operator at the Maria Isabel put her through to Jorge's room. The air-conditioned silence in the cave of the living room rose up around her like ice.

"*Bueno?*" Jorge answered. Even in that one word,

she heard the tiredness, the tension. She tried to picture his sharp, dark face, the face she could never wholly get to the other side of, the face whose darkness never fully lifted for her.

"Living it up?" she said.

There was a beat of silence while he relaxed. "Six women in here," he said. "All blond North Americans. *Gringas*, like you."

She forced lightness into her voice. "Then they'd better take credit cards."

"What's happened?"

"It's our turn now. Guadalupe says they moved onto the land during the night."

There was another beat. "I suppose that's a compliment. They held off on us until nearly the last."

"It's a compliment. They've always liked you."

"Was anybody hurt?"

"No, thank God. There was some damage." He wouldn't want to hear details now, and she wouldn't offer them. She knew him.

"Damage can be fixed."

"Any progress?" she asked.

"I've met a couple of senators." Read "bought" for "met," Kathleen thought. "But who knows how much influence they've got. Rumor has it that the government is behind the whole thing, anyway. It needs all the support it can get right now. Let a few landowners lose their land to some peasants and the government come down on the side of the peasants, and *viva la revolución*! Keeps the peasants out of the cities and the communists off the soapboxes, no?"

7

"Rumor has it, eh?"

"I know, Kathleen, I know." His voice sounded tired again. "That's why I haven't given up and come home yet. Who knows?"

"Who knows," she said. "Anything you want me to do?"

"Yes. Stay away from the country house. Don't hang around street corners with men waving red flags. Get to the border if it heats up too much—which may be now."

"No, not yet. It's all right in town so far."

"How's Luis?"

"He's fine," she said. "I think we'll forgo his therapist's appointment in Tucson this week. I can write a note and say, 'Dear Doctor Roth: Please excuse Luis's absence this week as there was a revolution.'"

"When I think of all the lovely Mexican women I could have married who show proper respect for the problems of the motherland . . ."

"You'd be bored utterly to death," she said. "I suppose you want Ramón to call you?"

"Yes. *Mira*, there is a thing you can do. If it's all right on the streets, go to the Club and get my mail."

"And open it?" she said. How big so many small things became here, she thought with an amazement that she supposed would never completely leave her. Jorge's mail at the Landowners Club. His "business" mail that didn't come to the house, all those parts of his life that he, that almost every Mexican man, "protected" his wife from. What secret deals, threats,

8

bribes, sometimes letters from women she'd suspected that mail of holding. But it had always been understood that he alone would pick it up, and she'd never questioned it. That was part of her conscious compromise with this place, with his life. She was impressed.

"And open it. I don't know when we'll be able to talk again—I don't know when I'll be able to get back here even to sleep again. But there may be things in it I need to know about."

"What kind of things?"

"If I knew, I wouldn't need to ask you to pick it up."

"Fair enough. Jorge?"

"*Sí?*"

"Thanks."

"For what?"

"You could have asked somebody else to pick it up. You could have asked Enrique."

"Enrique's my best friend, my *compadre*. You're my wife. It's not the same, *vida*. Not the same trust."

Again she was impressed. She'd been here long enough to know how many layers of *machismo* he had to fight through to be able to say that. "That's why I said thanks," she said. "You're coming around."

"Yanqui imperialist."

"Happy Independence Day," she said.

"What's that supposed to mean?"

"You should know. My Independence Day's the fourth of July. Mexico's comes on September sixteenth."

"Today's September sixteenth? So that's what all that damn noise outside is!"

"So the day's really been that frantic for you?"

"Yes, *vida*. That frantic."

"Don't worry about us here. The fort's being held down."

"Kathleen. Get out if you have to. Remember that."

"I will. I've got Luis, too. I won't forget."

"*Ten cuidado*. Take care. I love you."

"*Hasta pronto*," she said. "Until soon." The receiver clattered into place with sharp finality. Until soon, she thought, and the silence rose up around her again from the hard Mexican tiles.

New England tough, she thought, New England strong. When she turned from the phone, her hands crossed underneath her arms to keep them from trembling, she saw Luis standing in the door watching her. Was his endless silence friendly to him? she wondered as she knelt and held her arms out toward him. Or was there this fear in it for him, too?

It *has* been a good life, she thought as she squeezed Luis good-bye at the garage door—except for the loneliness, a good life. She loved her husband, her children. It had been harder since Luis had been born, but Guadalupe was always there to take care of the thousand details of running a house and caring for the children that her friends back home had to struggle with alone. She never touched a vacuum cleaner nor a garden hose—the other maids and the gardener handled all that. She could read for long hours if she wanted, write the poems that she only read to the cat, go with Jorge out to the country house for slow-paced weekends, drive awhile and ramble down the long, deserted beaches of the Gulf of California, explore the villages in the mountains and the jungles along the seacoast, fly to Tucson or San Diego for days of shopping and loving the sound of English. She missed that, too: she'd never have imagined you could be lonely for a language.

There had never been an absence of money; none of the balancing up of accounts at the end of the month to see if dinner out was possible—the kinds of things she would have faced if her husband were a junior executive or assistant professor back home. No, here two new cars and a pickup waited for her in the locked garage. The long, white modern house with plenty of glass took advantage of all the sun in this warm, dry valley. And the perfect lawn, the palms, the pool, the country club . . . But there were the walls around everything to keep the poor from seeing how you *really* lived, too. And the boredom. She knew she'd made choices, trade-offs.

Boredom? she thought as she backed the big Mexican Ford out into the street. A state police car sat on the corner, a watchdog for all these big, white, walled houses—some with barbed wire and watchtowers on the walls. The two blank-faced men in the car were on her side for now, she thought. She drew little comfort from that. Tomorrow, if these invasions did get out of hand, whose side would they be on? *They* didn't live in houses like these. She shuddered as she turned the corner under their flat eyes.

No boredom today. These past dozen years were a space without time for her. Only the children's growing up, the unwelcome surprise of discovering a new line or two in her face in the morning, broke the regular rhythm of the crops, the trips, the warm years without seasons. At first the notion that most of the vegetables people ate back home in the winter came from this Yaqui Valley, from this rich, irrigated land she was mistress of so much of, had given her a sense of excitement and purpose. She had been able to imagine her father, snowed in, surrounded by his books, his typewriter, his students' papers, those thin, well-published novels he wrote for other academics like himself. She had imagined him biting into a sandwich with a tomato on it that Jorge's land had grown. *That's* what I'm doing, she would imagine herself saying to him—people are eating because of us. And she could feel pride.

Then she learned about the lifeboats, and the gnawing worry, the despair beneath the boredom. She was in a country where there wasn't enough of anything. The tomatoes that Jorge sent north across the border for better prices were tomatoes the poor in Mexico couldn't afford. Every day there were more people to feed, and there was less land to go around. And where could all those unfed people go? North to the border for the braver. To the bursting cities for others, where no jobs waited. And now some spilled in desperation, she knew, onto land like Jorge's, where they squatted and hoped for the government to give them the land they claimed the Revolution had promised them seventy years ago.

A good life, then, and a terrible life, Kathleen thought as she circled the cool, tree-hung reservoir and aimed the Ford out onto Boulevard Juarez, Obregón's main street. But, she reminded herself again, her life, her only life now.

She comforted herself with the fact that she hadn't married Jorge because of this life. She'd married him because she'd fallen in love with him, just as she had fallen in love with the desert light on one of those late-sixties cross-country junkets everyone made, and had left home to finish college at Arizona. He had been an agriculture major, God forbid, and she a Spanish minor. There had been a party, some smiles at her attempts at Spanish, a proper Mexican courtship, and then this, everything leading somehow to this life, this day.

For blocks along the boulevard, tractors, combines—any kind of farm machinery that had wheels—were stationed like soldiers at attention, their noses pointing out into the street. And on each one of them was a black bow and a printed note: "In memory of the freedom and the property rights of the Mexican People." Some of the tractors and machinery were Jorge's. Pulled out of the fields when the peasants took over, kept out now until the peasants saw how impossible it would be to farm without the landowners.

Desperation, Kathleen thought. If the government could take the land, it could take the machines, too,

13

when it wanted. Could take whatever bites out of her life it pleased, like this hungry country.

Downtown, past the tiny blue and pink and turquoise grocery stores and bakeries and tortilla shops and auto upholsterers and taco stands, past the sprawling new motel where the American wholesale buyers stayed when they came to town, food stalls were going up for the Independence Day celebration. It would be different this year, she knew. Speeches would be more guarded, the parade full of peasant groups with their banners and chants. Too much tequila or *bacanora*, and it could turn angry, explosive.

Now, though, the town was still reasonably calm as she pulled up in front of the marble entranceway of the Landowners Club. Crowds of peasants, *campesinos*, stood patiently in line before the closed doors of the Agricultural Bank across the street, or down the block before various government offices they hoped might open to offer them advisers or money to buy seeds and equipment, Kathleen guessed. Lots of luck, she thought. In front of the government-backed peasants' union, more *campesinos*—in straw cowboy hats, blue jeans or patched khakis, faded shirts, worn boots or work shoes—stared at the food stands, argued listlessly, leaned against the windows, and waited for something to happen. Their women, in housedresses and plastic sandals, checked Kathleen, checked her blond hair, checked the car. She read both envy and hostility in their looks. She forced herself to meet their stares, then let her eyes roam past the spray-painted hammer and sickle signs on most of the buildings and stop on the white-jacketed boy who trotted out of the club to take her car.

"Just stay with it a minute, *por favor*," she said. "I'm only going for the mail."

The boy's flat Indian face ducked in a little bow, and he stationed himself importantly beside the car.

The street's noise collapsed into a carpeted hush as the heavy bronze doors whooshed shut behind her. The outside smells, the diesel fumes, the odors of tamales steaming over open fires, gave way to lemon-oil furniture polish and faint, leftover perfume. When Kathleen asked the piglet-chubby, dinner-jacketed man at the desk for her husband's mail, he looked surprised. He considered a moment, then apparently decided extraordinary times bred extraordinary events, shrugged, bowed, and scurried off into another room.

While he was gone, Kathleen did a brief round of the front of the club, hoping for somebody who could give her fresh news. The lobby was nearly deserted, the restaurant closed. At the door to the auditorium, a sign announced a Landowners and Employees Support Rally. She peeked in. Most of the people sitting solemnly and listening to some impassioned speech she recognized: friends of Jorge's, and so friends of hers. Weejuns and cashmere, wool pants and tailored skirts. Alligators over their hearts, spray in their hair. Uniforms, like the uniforms of the *campesinos* on the street outside. Not many employees in the bunch, she thought, unless maybe some accountants. A pang of

15

Vermont orneriness hit her, and she was as conscious of her own tailored clothes as if they'd had a scarlet letter sewn on them.

"Señora Zaragoza?"

With a start, she let the auditorium door click closed. The desk clerk stood at her elbow with a half dozen envelopes in his pudgy hand. He smiled. "Going to the rally?"

"I gave at the office," she said.

"Fine, fine," he said, still smiling as if he had not understood at all what she'd said. "Any news from Señor Zaragoza?"

"It's all going well." She took the envelopes from him nervously. "He says he has six blond women in his room and has bribed two senators already."

The man's smile froze. "Hah!" he said after a moment. Kathleen patted the pudgy hands he held clasped over his stomach and turned on her heel to go. She felt a little better.

She shuffled the envelopes as she crossed the lobby. Most of them had business return addresses, as she'd expected. But two of them stopped her: neither had postmarks. One was in a woman's hand, and the other had no return address at all. She turned and called to the desk clerk.

He was at her side again in seconds. "Señora?"

"Where did these letters come from?"

He took the envelopes from her and turned them over a few times, as if he could somehow see inside them that way. "By messengers, I imagine, señora," he announced.

"Messengers?"

"It's not uncommon." He smiled again, enjoying his revenge. "Sometimes there are private matters— very private. . . ."

"From everyone except you, no doubt." Weak, she thought. Weak, Kathleen.

Outside, she dug in her purse for a fifty-peso note to give to the boy who'd watched her car, then got in and switched on the air conditioning. Her urge was to open immediately the two letters without postmarks, but the faces staring at her from the sidewalks stopped her. She didn't know what she'd find in the letters. But whatever she found, she wanted to find in privacy, not in this glass display box of a car. Just in case.

In her bedroom she deliberately opened the business letters first. Nothing seemed out of the ordinary— letters from suppliers or buyers, bills. No reason except habit she could see for Jorge having them delivered to the club. She paused a moment before she opened either of the final two; she'd proved she could be strong enough to save them for last. Should she keep playing that game with herself? Oh, to hell with it. She ripped open the envelope in the woman's handwriting, noting that the return address was in a part of town she didn't think she'd seen twice in a dozen years.

The short letter was written on plain white typing paper. She glanced down at the signature first: Alicia

17

Dura. Dear Lord, she thought, "that communist woman."

"Sr. Zaragoza," it began, empty of all the rhetoric of most Spanish salutations. "We have taken note of your reasonableness and your past reputation. According to your wish, we will meet with you within the next seven days. It would please us greatly to talk as friends, not enemies."

That was all. She checked the date of the letter. September 8th. Seven days would have ended last night, the night their lands had been invaded. Jorge had left the morning of the ninth. She'd driven him to the airport. He hadn't stopped at the club for his mail. Apparently, if he'd been expecting this letter, it had come too late.

"To talk as friends." To talk about what as friends? Kathleen tried to remember the little she knew about Alicia Dura from the newspapers and the talk at the club. She was somewhere in her early thirties, near Kathleen's own age, and head of the radical Peasants Front in this part of the country. She'd apparently taken over for her father, who had been assassinated by gunmen sometime before Kathleen had married Jorge and come to Obregón. Kathleen had seen her picture in the papers—not bad looking, plainly dressed, eyes that faced the camera straight on. What on God's earth could she and Jorge have to *talk* about, as friends or otherwise?

The other letter intrigued her less. The address was carbon-ribbon typed and neat. A business letter of some sort, sent by messenger probably out of mistrust of the Mexican mails. When she opened it, she saw the signature was a man's, a name she'd never heard. And the clean typing on good bond paper confirmed her conclusion: a business deal Jorge wanted to keep to himself. She almost put it down and went back to Alicia Dura's letter, but Jorge had asked her to read them all.

"*Muy Estimado Sr. Zaragoza*," this one started, with all the flowery rhetoric in place, "Very Esteemed Sr. Zaragoza:

"Allow me to introduce myself. I am Juan Tomas Espinoza, a representative of the Sixteenth of September Game Committee."

No, Kathleen thought, Jorge won't care about this one—there's no gambler in him. But she read on.

"I write to inform you that you have been selected to participate in this year's Game. First, let me tell you something about yourself. Your wife is Kathleen, a North American who spends one month each year with her family in the town of Bristol, the State of Vermont, usually the month of June. Your two oldest children, Federico and Jaime, aged ten and eight, are in school near there at St. Francis Academy in the town of Montpelier. Their rooms are numbers six and twelve, respectively, in the Watson Memorial Dormitory. They ski on weekends in the winter, usually cross-country alone from their grandparents' house. Your youngest son is Luis, who is at home with your wife. Since he is a deaf-mute she takes him for therapy once a week to Tucson, in Arizona, to the office of a Dr. Harold Roth. The rest of the time he works with a local therapist named Teresa Mendez, on Calle Elias. You yourself, Sr. Zaragoza, are often away on business to Tucson, Nogales, and Los Angeles. In Tucson you prefer a restaurant called La Fuente, and have your dinners there almost exclusively. We will be glad to furnish other particulars of your life upon request in order to establish our sincerity.

"In five days, on September 16th, I will visit you at your home in Ciudad Obregón at two P.M. Please have two hundred and fifty thousand American dollars ready for me, in cash. I regret to have to inform you that if you do not choose to participate in the Game as I have specified, we will begin the next round of the Game by eliminating one of your children first, then continuing through the remainder of your family to yourself, at times and upon occasions convenient to the Game Committee. No alternative arrangements will be made available to you, Sr. Zaragoza. As you are aware, the Committee has a long-standing reputation for fairness. We sincerely hope this will be our only visit to you in your lifetime.

"I look forward to meeting you.

"Respectfully,
JUAN TOMAS ESPINOZA
Authorized Representative"

Her eyes rested on the even, businesslike signature, as if she were waiting for it to tell her something more. Then she numbly skimmed the text again to see if she'd missed anything. The sixteenth of September.

Today. At two o'clock. She glanced at the clock on her nightstand. In three and a half hours.

She dropped the letter on the bed and held her hands back away from it, as if she'd touched something filthy. Who knew all these things about herself and her family? How did they know them? Had they been watching her? When she believed she was alone with Luis or her thoughts, or in bed with Jorge at night, had there been somebody watching, making notes? And dear sweet Jesus, had they gone to her children's *dormitory*, seen them through the windows, talked to them, touched them?

A bubble of nausea rose to her throat, and she stood and took deep breaths until it was under control. Her eyes teared and she shoved the tears away angrily with the back of her hand.

How *dare* anybody invade her life that way, she thought. And then: they had dared and that was the fact—how they dared didn't matter in the least. And all the crying, all the disgust on earth wouldn't keep two o'clock from coming.

She looked at the letter again and made herself pick it up. It was not a joke—a hoax, maybe, but not a joke. Nobody went to all the trouble this letter writer had gone to for a joke. Whether there was something called the Sixteenth of September Game or not, the letter was real. Somebody had been in Vermont and in Tucson and here, watching, spying.

Then why didn't they know Jorge was in Mexico City? The letter was dated two days after Jorge left. Why didn't they know she didn't have the least idea

21

whether Jorge could raise a quarter of a million dollars, much less how to go about it herself—and in three and a half hours! On a national holiday, with a damned revolution about to happen!

When she picked up the receiver to dial Jorge's hotel, her fingers shook so much she had to try twice before the numbers came out right. As the hotel operator rang his extension, Kathleen let her eyes slip around the familiar bedroom. There were the closets, Jorge's clothes in one, hers in the other. There were the pictures of the children on the dresser beside her crystal perfume bottles, Jorge's carved jewelry box. On the walls there were the paintings she'd lived with for years, the Tamayo she'd so coveted the first time she'd gone to Mexico City with Jorge, the bright Mexican colors in all of them. And there were the equally bright flowers Guadalupe made sure were on the desk every day.

And from the phone, the dark, heavy ring that nobody was answering in Mexico City.

Familiar? she thought. Normal? That was the miserable joke—that she'd let herself be lulled by the years into thinking that such things could ever exist in this place.

"Page him," she told the operator. During the wait, she looked at the clock. Three minutes had gone by since she'd last looked! Three minutes out of three and a half hours. *Damn you*, Jorge, she thought. *Be there!*

She didn't let the operator finish her apology before she hung up and pushed the buzzer for Guadalupe.

She forced herself to count to sixty before she buzzed again. Control. Control.

Guadalupe's sandals slapped through the door. Luis was hanging on to her dress and sliding along the tiles. When he saw Kathleen, he let go and ran to the bed and jumped in with her.

She studied Luis's face a moment. He seemed happy. But his eyes, so brown they were almost black, were Jorge's. They hid things from her, the way Jorge's unconsciously did. "Having a good time?" she signed to him in their private, shorthand version of the "official" sign language he used with his therapists. There were so many things between them that needed only a hint of meaning for both of them to understand, and she'd always felt closer to him because of that, had always felt somehow more part of his closed world. He nodded and smiled. She pulled him to her and hugged him fiercely. To eliminate her youngest son, the letter had said, *eliminate*.

"Lupe, what does today mean to you?" she made her voice say.

"Sixteenth of September, señora? Independence Day from the Spaniards, no? When Father Hidalgo down at Dolores rang the bells and . . ."

"No. Not that."

Guadalupe looked bewildered.

"Is there some sort of game?" Kathleen went on. "Something called the Sixteenth of September Game?"

Guadalupe looked bewildered a moment more, then gathered her round face up in thought. "There was something once in the newspapers, I think."

23

"What?"

"I don't know, señora. Something once a long time ago. I read it."

"Just—does it really exist? Remember at least that much."

"Would it be in the newspapers if it didn't exist, señora? I think people win money or something."

It was pointless. Guadalupe was always an encyclopedia of misinformation. Kathleen eased her arms from around Luis and sat him on the bed beside her. In a normal world, she would call the police, she thought. Show them the letter, have them get in touch with Jorge. But what was one of the first things Jorge had taught her about Mexico? Stay away from the police. Pray they never come to you about anything. Never go to them. And where in God's name *was* Jorge?

She flung herself off the bed, and Luis looked startled. "We're going out, Lupe. Luis and I are going out."

"To the parade, señora? Oh, I think today . . ."

"No, not to the parade. If anyone calls for me, I've just gone *out. Comprendes?*"

She didn't wait for Guadalupe's worried look to compose itself. She held out her hand, and Luis slid off the bed to take it.

Out. Now the urge to get in the car and simply drive was almost overwhelming. Head north, think of the border. It was so close, so painfully close.

But if the letter was from who it said it was, surely today of all days she was being watched. If she drove toward the border, how far would she get? She turned back and snatched up the letter, and the note from Alicia Dura. Why she took both of them she didn't know. But there was something almost comforting in the honest, plain handwriting of Alicia Dura's letter, something that softened the hard, even lines of the other.

Out. If not to the police, if not toward the border, then to Enrique's sprawling house. Jorge's *compadre*, that Spanish word which meant more "brother" than "friend." That much she understood about Mexico: if she went to her husband's *compadre*, he would take her in, no questions. And he would know if this "Game Committee" really existed.

She decided to walk the block to Enrique's house. She felt safer that way. The state police were still on the corner, and if she had to, she could see another car coming from far enough away to duck into a gate or some bushes.

She checked the street carefully from behind the wrought-iron garden gate before she stepped out into it. There was only the aging tan police Chevrolet with its cracked taillight and the blank faces inside the windows, open now against the growing midday heat. She tried not to look at them as she and Luis passed on the other side of the street. Where was she being watched from, *where*?

Enrique's maid opened the door for them as soon as she heard Kathleen's accent. Enrique hadn't gone to Mexico City with Jorge's committee: Jorge didn't trust his temper or his reputation with the liberals.

His gunmen, his *pistoleros*, were notorious—they were a private police force, a private army on his lands, and the peasants hated them. His was one of the houses with barbed wire on the walls and with watch-towers his gunmen sat in through long afternoons, cigarette smoke rising, rifle barrels catching the sun. "What's yours is yours only as long as they don't take it away from you," she'd heard him tell Jorge. And he meant it.

The life of someone like Enrique was another of Mexico's contradictions, she realized as she waited in the foyer for Enrique's wife to be called. This house was a place of peace inside, an island behind the gun towers. Cool whites and blues, just the right light from just the right angles to catch the sculpture and paintings, adobe tiles and woven rugs on the floors. And with his friends, Enrique was generous to a fault. His dinners were the best in the state, he gave money to every charity that asked, he was a decent father and so far as she knew, a better husband than most. The radical newspapers had called him a barbarian, but was this man in a white cardigan, smiling, with just touches of gray around his temples, this clear-eyed man in studious glasses who came toward her behind his wife with his hand out, a barbarian? Where did you have to look at him from to think he was a barbarian? She wished she knew; she might need a barbarian now.

"*Qué milagro!* What a miracle!" his wife, Concha, said, moving loosely in a blue satin pants suit. "We thought we'd lost you—thought you might have jumped ship."

"Nope. I've signed on for the duration," Kathleen said and forced a smile. Enrique took her hand while Concha knelt and made exaggerated welcoming motions to Luis. Luis decided to play shy and circled Kathleen's leg.

"What news from Mexico City?" Enrique asked as he led her toward the patio. Luis trailed her like a third leg, smiling now at Concha's clown faces but not yet fully convinced to give up his shyness. But when Concha veered off toward the kitchen, he followed her. She always kept some special treat there for him, and he knew it. Kathleen was glad his shyness had lost to his stomach. It would be easier to talk to Enrique without Concha. Her sympathizing would be too much to deal with. "We're having a late breakfast on the patio. Join us?" Enrique said.

Kathleen thanked him, but no. She sat and quickly gave him what little news she had, and he shook his head.

"I was out at my lands this morning," he said as he sprawled into a patio chair. "I have some of them back. During the night, poof!—the *campesinos* went away. Left everything they had behind them."

"Enrique . . ." There was no time now, no time for any of that.

"Jorge should come home, you know. Be with his men. That's the way the land comes back. The only way."

"Enrique," she tried again. "Have you ever heard

of something called the Sixteenth of September Game?''

He hesitated, drew in a breath. *"Sí."*

"Does it really exist?"

"Sí."

Her own breath shortened, and her stomach felt cold. "Can you tell me what you know about it?"

"Why?"

She handed him the letter. He opened it and scanned it, then gave it back to her. He took off his glasses and passed his hand across his eyes. "I'm very sorry," he said. "Jorge should be here."

"He's not," she said. "Tell me about it."

"It's very old, back to the time of the Revolution, I suppose. They came to see my father once. He played, and they never came back. A friend of his didn't play. He tried to take his family to Arizona."

She waited for him to go on. "And?"

"They found him. After only one child, he played." Enrique must have seen her body tense; he leaned toward her and covered her hand with his. *"Mira,* Kathleen. I have to tell you that, *no?"*

"Yes. Yes, you do," she said. She let his hand stay, drawing comfort from it the way she had from Alicia Dura's letter, but looked beyond him at the reflections from the pool dancing on the palms, the perfect green of the lawn, the rainbow colors of the bird of paradise flowers, the delicate orange blossoms of the bottlebrush trees, the magenta bougainvilleas. And then at the stark guard towers that gave the lie to it all. "What should I do?"

"What did Jorge say?"

"I can't reach him."

"But you said you talked to him."

"Before I got the letter."

"Ah," he said. He took his hand away and placed it stiffly on his knee.

"What if I can't reach him before two o'clock?"

"You have to reach him."

"You're his *compadre*, Enrique."

"I am. What are you asking me for, Kathleen?"

"Apart from what's invested in the land—does Jorge have a quarter of a millon dollars? That he could get to?"

"With his hardware stores, and the houses in Tucson . . . yes, I think so."

"Do you?"

"In cash?" He gave her a sad, patient smile. "It's all over there," he said, waving vaguely toward the border. "I tried to get Jorge to send his out, too, when all the devaluations and land troubles started. He's too stubborn for himself sometimes. You know that. 'I'll be all right,' he said to me. 'I'm staying here. If Mexico's good enough for me, it's good enough for my money.' "

"Can you get it from somebody else?"

"Kathleen." He covered her hand again. This time the touch was less comforting. "Listen to me. Everybody, *everybody* but Jorge has gotten their money out of the country. If I could help you, if I could go from door to door and beg the money for you, I would. But the only man in all of Obregón who could even possi-

29

bly have that much cash is Jorge. I've got maybe five hundred dollars—and you know that's yours if you want it."

"Five hundred dollars," she said flatly. From the patio door she heard Concha babbling at Luis. Sometimes she thought Concha believed that if you just kept talking at Luis long enough, he'd eventually understand. Suddenly she wanted Concha's sympathy after all, wanted her to come and take her hands and cry for her, because she couldn't. And suddenly, too, she was very angry at herself for her own ignorance. Here she was, finding out even the most essential things she should know about her husband's affairs from his best friend. And all because of those stupid conscious compromises she'd made when she'd married him: not to embarrass him, not to be the pushy North American woman who meddled in her husband's business, let it go because you love him, sink into Mexico, you've made your choice, Kathleen, now live with it. Shame joined her anger when she asked Enrique, "Where would Jorge's money be, if he had that much."

Her face must have shown what was happening in her. "It's all right," he said. "It's probably best you didn't know."

"No, damn it, it's not probably best! Where does my husband keep our money?"

He was surprised, probably embarrassed. He put his glasses on again to gain a moment. He cleared his throat and tried to sound paternal. "Some in the bank. Enough to make it look good to the government in case they want to know where he gets his dollars to do business in the States."

"I know about that money," she said. A small victory. "There can't be more than ten thousand dollars."

"No, there wouldn't be. As for the rest . . ." He shook his head. "When I told him he ought to send his dollars out of the country, he got upset with me. We haven't talked about it since."

"In a safe-deposit box?"

"No. Not since the government has nationalized the banks."

"My God, my God," she said. "What should I think, Enrique—that my husband has buried his money somewhere like a pirate in a bad movie?"

"Nothing is normal now, Kathleen. Understand that. People don't do normal things."

"Normal?" In spite of herself, her hands balled into tight, nervous fists. The word again. Was it normal or not normal in Mexico that you so distrusted your own government's money that you kept everything you had in dollars and then lived in fear that the government was going to confiscate your dollars along with the banks? Was it normal that some macabre "game" had been operating for seventy years and people like Enrique described it to her the way he might describe rain? She looked at her watch. Twenty minutes were gone. She pushed sharply to her feet. "Then what if I can't reach Jorge, Enrique? I can explain to them, can't I?"

He shook his head and avoided her eyes. "No."

She was conscious that her voice was rising toward hysteria. "No? Of course I can."

"It won't matter to them. They have rules."

"How do you know—how do you know so much about this miserable damn 'game'?"

"Jorge would know about it, too. We all do."

"I don't—and I thought I was part of *we*. Who are they? Who is this Game Committee?"

"That I don't know. Nobody does."

"And you put up with it."

"We've been putting up with things for a long time in Mexico, Kathleen. We've learned about putting up with things. *Mira*, you've just got to find the money. Or Jorge. I have to make you understand that . . ."

"Help me, Enrique. Please."

"I'll telephone people. Anybody I know in Mexico City who might help find him." He still wasn't meeting her eyes.

"Let us stay here until we do—you can do that, can't you?"

"No."

"For the love of God, Enrique . . ."

"Kathleen—I have children, too. And mine are in school in Hermosillo—in Mexico, not a long way away in Vermont. Please—please understand me. If you try to cheat at the game and they find out I helped you . . ."

She swept her hand toward the guard towers. "And what about those?"

"Those? Those are no good, not for this. I know the game, Kathleen. I know the rules. *Por Dios*,

32

believe me. You can't get away from it. *You* can't, *I* can't."

He said the last with such compressed violence that she backed away from him. He stood, and went on. "Jorge would do the same thing. Jorge would understand."

She kept backing away until she felt her heel catch on a patio brick and she nearly stumbled. When she got her balance back, she spun around and away from him. Without putting it in words, she understood the violence: he was afraid, and he hated himself for his fear—and maybe her for witnessing it. Her eyes hazed with tears as she ran toward the patio door. Through the haze she saw Concha in the door, frozen with astonishment, Luis's hand in hers. She brushed past her and scooped Luis up in her arms. She was halfway through the living room when she heard Enrique's voice calling after her, "Find Jorge. Find the money. I'll do what I can. Trust me." And then at the door, "I'll call you. You've got my word."

Outside, the shadows of the watchtowers had almost been sucked back up into the white concrete of their walls as the sun arced into midday. She kept running, feeling the heat from the asphalt of the pavement searing through her thin soles. In the battered tan police car, the two blank faces turned, impassive as desert birds, to watch her.

While Kathleen tried to phone Jorge's empty hotel room again, Guadalupe's busy hands fluttered around the edges of her vision like dust motes in the sun: now with a cold towel, now with a mug of manzanilla tea—"for the nerves," she whispered—now with a glass of milk and a book for Luis. Luis wanted to go back to his room, but Kathleen, knowing she wasn't being reasonable, wouldn't let him leave her bedroom. There was no window onto the street from there, no way for him to be seen by anyone but herself and Guadalupe.

When she'd come in with Luis, her face tear streaked and with beads of sweat already dotting her forehead, she'd told Guadalupe something vague about bad news from Mexico City that Enrique had given her. No need to involve Guadalupe, not yet. The poor woman was already involved in enough, with the land problems. Before the day was out, only heaven knew what else she would have to face. Most of all Kathleen needed her busy presence now, her routine to bolster her.

And it was working. Kathleen looked at the clock, without panic this time, and saw she had three hours yet. She closed her eyes and concentrated on her breathing. Slowly, in, out, in, out. And she slipped into her trick again—for a few seconds, a minute, no more. She supposed there might be something vaguely mystical about her trick, if her common sense had ever let her consider doing anything mystical. She had discovered it sometime into her second year in Mexico, when the newness had worn off and she began to realize she lived in a glass bowl among Jorge's people with no place to hide. The trick was this: she changed the quality of the light inside her head. She imagined the pond at the summer house in the Green Mountains on an August afternoon, with the light soft from a hazy New England sky, the spruces and maples and birches tinging the light with deep, soft green—at least in her imagination. She listened to the soughing of the breeze in all that green, promising the evening's cool, promising a fire in the fireplace, even in August. She listened to the silence of the woods, a silence that only seemed to be without sound because of the absence of human noise. And she would forget dust for a little while, forget this Sonoran light that always *felt* red. And when she opened her eyes again, it was as if she'd been thirsty and had a drink of cold, sweet water from the spring behind the cabin, as she'd done on August afternoons when she was a girl. She had been herself again for a while, had been who she'd always thought she was going to be. And she had been able to face the red light of the seasonless valley again.

But today she couldn't get there. Today the red light receded only slightly, but it wouldn't entirely go away.

Find the money, Enrique had said. Find Jorge. She understood Enrique's fear; in Mexico there were times when you commended your friends to God, lit a candle, and saved yourself. But she knew also that she was still angry, that something had changed between herself and Enrique's family forever.

She opened her eyes and found Luis, sitting with his book in Jorge's easy chair. Luis was here, but her other two children weren't. And no matter how much there was to fear here in Obregón, to try to do, she had to face what might happen to her other sons after today.

She reached for the phone and dialed the code for the United States, then for Vermont. When her father answered, she cut off his usual surprise and pleasantries as quickly as she could. It took an effort: the sound of his voice was a temptation to let go that she had to avoid at all costs.

She knew what would happen if she tried to explain the game to him—the disbelief, the tacit blame for being in such a mad place, all the rational solutions that would be of no more use here than computers to buffalos. She made up something about a kidnap threat against the children, something he could understand from the evening news, yet something frightening enough to make him take her seriously.

"I want you to pick up Federico and Jaime now, Dad. Before dinner. Don't tell the school where you're taking them—don't tell anyone. Bring Mother with you if you can. And don't come back home, at least not until I talk to you again." She could see her father's worried face, almost hear him thinking. She held her breath. They'd fought often, and he'd lectured her more often. But when there was a real crisis, real need, there was an understanding between them: ask questions later, argue later, but face the crisis together now. She prayed that somehow her voice had made this crisis real enough for him in that place where such horrors existed only on television screens. He sighed heavily, and said simply, "Of course."

She let her breath out silently and thanked God for the power of simple lies.

"And call the police, Dad. Tell them what I told you. Let them know where you are so I can find you."

"Your police there are on top of this, I hope," he said. "I'll have someone here get in touch with them. And you contact the American consulate, if you haven't already. I want you to do that right away."

"Of course, yes—have somebody be in touch with the police here. And don't worry. We'll be fine. They've got everything under control."

"And the consulate."

"I'll do that, Dad. I'll get right over to the capital and do it."

When she hung up, she put the phone down as reluctantly as if the cord had been a lifeline from a boat too far to reach. She'd been talking to another planet.

She tried Jorge's room again. Nothing. She'd been home ten minutes now.

"Guadalupe!" she called.

Guadalupe must have been just outside the door; she was in the room almost before the echo of Kathleen's voice had stopped.

"Has Señor Jorge hidden anything here in the house? Anything that you know of? Or even outside the house—has he buried anything?"

Guadalupe's pursed lips disapproved again. "Señor Jorge never hides anything from his family, señora."

"Not from us. From other people."

Guadalupe's expression didn't change. "Señora. What is it? What do you want me to help you find?"

Kathleen hesitated, then said, "Money, Guadalupe. Dollars."

"*Muchos?*"

"Yes, a lot. Probably boxes full."

"And you need them now," Guadalupe said, a statement, not a question, with a hint of distrust in it. "While Señor Jorge is away."

"Do you know where they are? For God's sake, tell me."

Guadalupe studied her a moment, struggling. "Is it for the land, señora? Will it help save the land?" There was hope, almost a plea, in her voice.

"Yes," Kathleen said. "Yes, it's for the land."

"Ah!" Guadalupe's round face settled into relief. "Let me think."

"Then you *don't* know."

"Señora, I don't know, no. But I might guess."

"Where?"

"Not here. I know all of this house. If it was in the garden somewhere, the gardeners would have told me. But I will tell you something, something that I've kept in my mind a long time. Once, when Señor Jorge was still a student in the *preparatorio* and his mother and father were still alive . . ." She crossed herself. ". . . we were at the country house and a pipe broke in the ground beneath the floor. Ramón and I

38

were just married then, and Señor Jorge's father had Ramón dig up the floor beside the old washstand in the kitchen. I don't know if Señor Jorge's father knew what he would find or not—his grandfather had built the house when he was still a baby. But under the washstand, when they moved it, there was a paving stone that they lifted out of the way. And underneath that was a concrete box with a lid on it made out of iron and a key in it. Señor Jorge's father told us that many people who had some money during the Revolution had places like that made where they could hide things from Pancho Villa's men. I remember that after Ramón had quit digging for the day, Señor Jorge came back into the kitchen while I was making dinner, and he stooped down and took the key out of the iron lid. Then he looked at me and winked and put the key in his pocket. 'You never know, Guadalupe,' he said to me, and ever since, I've remembered that. You want me to guess? That's what I guess.''

And the country house might as well be in Cuba, Kathleen thought. Only twenty-five minutes away, and from what she knew she'd be turned back before she got within a mile of it. All week the papers had been full of the pictures of the other landowners' properties: barricades across the roads leading to them, armed men and women crowding into trucks beside the barricades, fists raised. And what would she do—drive up and explain to them that there might be a concrete box full of dollars hidden in the house, and would they please let her go take the dollars out before they got to them?

"He doesn't carry a key like that now," she said to Guadalupe. "Have you seen it since?"

"Once or twice, señora. And only at the country house. It's probably there somewhere, but only Señor Jorge would know where."

And you could look for a month through all those buildings out there and never find it, Kathleen knew. No, she'd have to forget the key. "Have you talked to Ramón again? Has anything changed at the country house?"

Guadalupe shook her head. "He called me. It's worse, señora. There are even more of them now. He couldn't get in. Nobody can."

Kathleen felt the chill creep up on her again in the house's silence after the sound of Guadalupe's voice had stopped, the chill that came to rest in her stomach somewhere. All right, she thought. That chill was nothing compared to a Vermont winter. How many of those had she survived? And how well she'd forgotten that you had to survive, living so long and so easily in this place of red light. Mexico had its rules. This Game Committee had its rules. And her rules? Had she given up the right to make any rules of her own these past dozen years? Damn them, damn rules that smothered you, terrorized you, murdered you.

"Yes," she said. "Yes, somebody can get in."

"No, señora," Guadalupe said. Then, when Kathleen didn't answer her, "I'll call somebody and see if I can find Ramón."

"No. I won't need Ramón—even if you could find him. Get me a pair of jeans and one of Jorge's work shirts. Go quick." She began to slip out of her skirt and blouse, her open-toed shoes and stockings. Guadalupe, apparently warned by her voice, didn't argue. She began rifling Jorge's closet and came out with a plaid cowboy shirt, then dove into Kathleen's closet. "And a pair of sandals."

When she was down to her panties and bra, she went and knelt beside Luis's chair, and touched him to get his attention. "I'm going out for a little while," she signed to him. "I want you to stay in here and let Guadalupe bring you whatever you need. All right?"

"I don't want to," he signed back. His face showed what he couldn't say, his sense that something was wrong that the mystery of the noisy adult world wouldn't let him understand.

"I'm going to do something to help daddy. I'll be right back."

He frowned, and signed reluctantly, "Okay."

She gave him a hug that he accepted with equal reluctance, then signed to him, "I love you."

Be safe, my son, she thought. Whatever it takes for that, I'll do.

When she took the clothes from Guadalupe, their hands touched briefly. Kathleen glanced down at her still-slim body and saw that it was almost as brown as Guadalupe's hand, from the many hours she'd spent by the pool. That wasn't her body; her skin was white and soft from living under pullovers and flannel shirts to fight the New England chill. She had to remember that now, keep remembering who she had been, who she had to be again.

As she pinned her long hair back she told Guadalupe once more that she was to stay in this room with Luis, and that she would be back in no more than an hour and a half. If she wasn't, Guadalupe was to take Luis and get into the police car outside. And to stay there no matter what—if she had to, she should make such a scene that the police would have to take her to the *comandancia* office. Guadalupe nodded, certain of her ground. Making scenes with policemen would be no problem.

Kathleen squeezed Luis's hand good-bye. As she turned for the door, the phone rang. She signaled for Guadalupe to answer it. "I'll take it only if it's Señor Jorge," she said.

Guadalupe answered, then put her hand over the mouthpiece. "It's Señor Enrique," she whispered.

"Find out what he wants."

Guadalupe asked, then listened a minute. "He wants to know if you've heard from Señor Jorge."

"Tell him no. But tell him I'm going to the country house. He'll understand."

She left before giving Enrique a chance to answer. He couldn't help her now. She dismissed him.

She pulled into a space marked Vice-Comandante Only in front of the faceless, modern, concrete police *comandancia*. A traffic policeman watched with such amazement that she was able to slip out of the car and into the building's foyer before he could even bring his whistle to his mouth. She wouldn't stop now. If she stopped, she might start thinking, doubting. Not going to the police was Jorge's rule—Jorge's and Enrique's and other men like themselves. Police for them meant bribes, meant corruption, meant bureaucracy that took years to make nothing at all happen. They settled things quickly and neatly without the police. But that was their way, not hers today. If it took bribes, she would bribe. If it meant entangling herself in a bureaucracy for years, she would worry about those years after today. She had only a little over two and a half hours. Surely, surely there would be one reasonable man among all those who faced her from desks and behind counters in the big, dingy, typewriter-noisy room before her.

She stopped in front of a tall man in the green uniform of the *federales* who looked up at her expectantly from a counter at the end of the room. He wore sergeant's stripes, and his uniform was tailored so that it fit him as tightly as a wet suit. "Señora?" he said.

"I want to see Comandante Aguilar." She said it with as much authority as she could muster. She would start with Aguilar; she had met him at Jorge's country club a few times, had had brief, empty talks with his wife and himself at cocktail parties. Jorge had made certain they met. While you didn't go to the police if you could help it, you still kept on the good side of the local chief of the *federales* whenever you could. She remembered him as a seemingly intelligent, quiet man with a thin, neatly moustached face that didn't seem to reveal either cruelty or kindness. He was a cipher to her, a blind chance.

"Your name, señora?" the tailored uniform asked.

"Kathleen Zaragoza. The wife of Jorge Zaragoza. Tell the comandante it's urgent."

She saw a flicker of recognition in the sergeant's eyes when she gave her name, but he turned meaningfully to look at the mournful people ranged along the bench outside the door marked Comandante. Yes, señora, the look said, they're all urgent. Kathleen faked the arrogance that she knew was expected of families like Jorge's when they were dealing with "inferiors." "The comandante will see me," she said. "Please tell him immediately that I'm here." And please, God, let it work, she said to herself.

The uniform nodded briefly and crossed the depressing dun tiles to the comandante's door. He rapped once and went in without waiting for an answer.

Kathleen didn't want to meet the eyes of the people on the bench, some of whom had probably been waiting since dawn. Or since last week. She turned back to the two rails that formed the aisle she'd walked down to reach the sergeant's desk, to the sea of nicked and peeling desks that a score of people sat behind—some in uniform, some not—clacking out reports in triplicate on old manual typewriters, to the dusty eagle-and-serpent Mexican flag on the wall, the photos of the *Presidente* with his red sash of office, the torn posters with valiant slogans about work and the motherland on them. At one end of the room a cluster of men, *campesinos*, stood with two armed *federales* loosely guarding them. They watched her coldly. One of the men was bleeding from a cut underneath his hairline. All of them had torn and muddy clothes. With a shock of recognition, she realized that these were the people she would be facing at the country house, people who had stood in police stations like this off and on for years, as battered from police pistol butts and riot clubs as these men. This was *their* Mexico. She felt a rush of sympathy for them, and knew she was afraid of them, too.

"Señora?" The tailored sergeant was holding a wooden gate in the counter open for her, and the door to the comandante's office was ajar. The people on the bench studied the swirls on the tiles as she went by.

Comandante Aguilar rose from his chair and held out his hand when she came in. His office was as depressing as the rest of the place, even though there was a carpet on the floor and red draperies hung at the windows. There was no warmth, nothing but file cabinets and posters and framed certificates that signaled "official." Aguilar offered her an official smile and directed her to a plastic-covered swivel chair in front of his desk. He ran through a few pleasantries about how good it was to see her again, and how was her family, and then, with the slightly pained air of a busy Mexican gentleman indulging the problems of a woman, asked how he could be of help.

"I want to get to our country house," she said.

He blinked. "On your husband's farmlands?"

"Yes."

"The ownership of those lands is in dispute now, señora."

"I don't care about those. I want to get to our country house."

"But you have to pass through the farmlands to get to the house, correct?"

"Yes. Of course."

"And therein lies the problem, señora. I have orders not to allow any of the owners—or perhaps former owners—onto their lands for the time being. For their own safety and for the sake of public order. You understand, no?"

"Then fly me over the lands in a helicopter. I don't care."

He gave her a perfunctory I-know-you're-not-serious smile.

"Comandante Aguilar," she said, "I'm asking you as a man, as the father of a family, for help. Please." Anything it takes, she'd secretly promised Luis. She knew the words, attitude, that Mexican women used in desperation to manipulate men when all else failed. She'd never had to use them with Jorge, and had sworn she never would.

He thought a moment. "Why is it so urgent that you reach that house, Señora Zaragoza? I would like to understand."

She opened her handbag and pulled out the letter from the Game Committee. And damn the rules, she reminded herself. My rule is that when you have nothing to lose, don't stop to think about rules. The letter from Alicia Dura caught in a fold of the Game

Committee's envelope as she slipped it from her bag. It fluttered to the floor and she scooped it up, she hoped before Aguilar could get a look at it.

Aguilar's face didn't change as he read the letter. When he finished, he handed the letter back and said, "And your need to get to your country house has to do with this letter."

She'd expected if not sympathy, then at least surprise, some recognition of her urgency. "Yes, Comandante."

"And it has to do with the funds requested."

The funds requested, she thought, the flat way a banker would say it! "Yes."

"You are aware, señora, of the laws prohibiting possession of unreported foreign currency. This country must have those currencies to pay its foreign debt."

God in heaven, she thought. "Comandante, you read the letter. Please."

He didn't answer for a long moment. All right, Kathleen thought, try it all. "You know my husband has other funds—legal ones. He has businesses, even if the lands are gone. If you'd like to discuss an investment . . ."

He waved his hand to cut her off. "That isn't the question now, señora." There was no offense taken. A bribe was normal, was ordinary business. "I want you to do as I tell you. I want you to return to your home. I want you to stay there until I can authenticate that letter. And then I will put myself in touch with you."

47

"Comandante, I only have two and a half hours. . . ." she began, then stopped herself. "You said, authenticate this letter?"

"*Sí.*"

"How can you authenticate it?"

"I want you to return home, señora. *Por favor.*" His eyes held hers steadily.

Once, as a girl, she'd leapt from a high tree limb into the lake. She'd hit the water wrong, and lost her breath. She remembered the feeling now, the cold lake water swirling up around her, her vision darkening, the terrible sensation of not being able to make her lungs function. She pushed herself up from the chair. "How can you authenticate this letter, Comandante? Who are you going to authenticate it with?"

Aguilar came around the desk toward her. She backed away. "Sergeant," Aguilar called. Then again, "Sergeant."

The sergeant from the counter swung in, saw Kathleen's face, and, waiting, looked to the comandante.

"Help Señora Zaragoza to her car," Aguilar said. "Take her through the side door."

The sergeant moved to take Kathleen's elbow. She recalled the blood coming from the face of the *campesino* in the office outside, and let him take it. Aguilar looked relieved. "With the troubles, señora," he said. "I have no one to send to your home with you. I'm sorry."

Kathleen started to speak, then shook her head.

"Understand me, señora," he went on. "Until I

contact you, there is no good you can do yourself, no place you can go to help yourself. Stay at home."

Kathleen nodded. She glanced at the comandante's face a last time to try to find some other message there. There was none. It was composed, as official as his pressed green uniform, the certificates on his wall, the captain's bars on his shoulder.

The sergeant called off the traffic policeman, who was confiscating her license plates outside, and helped her gently but firmly into the car. She drove away without looking back at him. Her shock propelled her through the gathering parade crowds as if the Ford were a tank: people scattered, raised fists at her. She didn't care. In each face, she saw someone watching her from the Game Committee. Was all of Mexico part of the thing? Where did it stop? It was like the Aztec image of the serpent swallowing its own tail: the whole country fed on itself, devoured itself, according to the whims of some invisible men in some unknown place, like the old gods who had demanded human sacrifice. And now was it Luis's turn, her turn?

She swung around the *zócalo*, the city's plaza, and saw crowds already gathering for the parade. On the bandstand a man stood and hacked the air with his hands as a crowd of students waved placards and tried to get red-bordered banners in place. Gawking *campesinos* packed the beds of old pickups and sucked on Coca-Colas or shoved things to eat at their children.

Go home. And what if the letter was "authenticated"? Would Aguilar suddenly have the authority to get her into the country house? And in time? He was a local police comandante—how long would it take him to get the authority to do *anything*, either from the government or the Game Committee? There was a terror in the slow mysteries of Mexico's bureaucracies, both secret and open, far greater than guns, greater than those crowds on the *zócalo* behind her.

Was that what he expected her to go home and wait for? No, oh no.

Her eyes on the road home, she fumbled in her purse for Alicia Dura's letter. She had one place left to go now, only one place where there were no bureaucracies or Game Committees. She was icily conscious that what she was about to do was an act of absolute desperation, maybe even madness. But the word "negotiate" kept coming back to her from the woman's letter, like a faint code message tapped out on the wall of this room she was in with nothing but doors that led nowhere.

Negotiate? She would negotiate with the devil himself if she had to now, for any kind of deal she could strike and with anything she had to put on the table. No matter what it cost her.

As soon as she came in, she tried Jorge again from the hall phone. Guadalupe watched her quietly until she slapped the receiver down into the cradle.

"No?" Guadalupe said. She stood with her hands folded, subdued, her worry taking a form Kathleen hadn't seen in her before.

"No." Kathleen crossed the hall and hugged her tightly for a moment.

"It's very serious, señora, no?" Guadalupe said.

"Very serious, *sí*."

"You're back quickly."

"I'm going out again. Is Luis all right?"

"He's asleep."

"Poor kid." She started for the bedroom. "I've got to wake him. He's going with me."

"To the country house? Please, señora . . ."

"No, not to the country house. I don't think so, anyway." Guadalupe followed her to the bedroom, where Luis was curled up in his father's armchair. His book was a tent on the floor at his feet. She touched him gently, and his eyes opened, closed, then opened again. When she was sure he was awake, she lifted him and stood. His face was still full of sleep, and the happiness of the morning was gone. He was angry with her, she thought, angry because something from her unknown world was happening that he was locked out of. She didn't blame him. She knew what it was like.

"Guadalupe," she said as she carried him from the room. "*Ojalá*, I ought to be back by two. If something happens and I'm not, someone may come by, a man. If he does, let him in and make him comfortable and ask him to wait. Tell him I'll be here as soon as I can."

"He's somebody about the land?"

"Yes. You should be all right with him. His business is with me."

"His name is Espinoza?"

She turned sharply. "How did you know that?"

"He telephoned, señora. He said he wanted to confirm his appointment at two."

"And what did you tell him?"

Guadalupe backed away a step. "I just took the message, señora. He had a good voice." She looked as if she were about to break into tears.

"Fine," Kathleen said, gentling her own voice. "That's all right—I'm just on edge. Everything's okay, and I'll be back by two. Everything's okay, no?"

Guadalupe nodded.

She saw Kathleen and Luis to the garage, and stayed to watch them go. By the time the battered tan police car pulled out to follow them, she was lowering the garage door.

Kathleen had seen the car jerk when its driver dropped it into gear as she turned the corner. By the time she'd reached the end of the block at Enrique's house, she saw it squarely in her rear-view mirror. She turned at the next corner, though she didn't need to. The police car turned. Kathleen reached across and fastened Luis's seat belt. She never fastened it except on the highway, and he looked puzzled.

"Going for a ride," she signed to him, and managed a smile.

Luis settled into the seat. Yes, a ride—somewhere, she thought. Your fear could become like your shadow, she decided. Sometimes bigger, sometimes smaller, but always there with you, so that you got used to it. And then you didn't think about it, so it didn't paralyze you. She wanted to get used to it, had to get used to it—soon. She checked the address on Alicia Dura's envelope. And when she pulled out onto Boulevard Juarez from her neighborhood side street, she turned the opposite way, toward downtown. The shadow of her fear grew a little longer as she sped up.

If she headed away from town, north toward the border, the men in the car would surely stop her. This way, she might be going back to the *comandancia*, for all they knew. They would wait and see. This would give her a little time and space.

Obregón was flat as a sea, a manufactured town in the middle of these endless miles of irrigated, fertile fields. Jorge had first described it to her as Mexico's Imperial Valley. It was a new town, built mainly after the Revolution by the European and American settlers who came in to open it up to their combines and tractors and schemes for dams and irrigation canals. Their names still marked the concrete, historyless stores and buildings downtown: Robinson, Brown, Bours. And as Mexican towns went, it was a rich town, a place of broad streets and evenly spaced blocks, of gleaming Ford and GMC and Datsun and VW and International Harvester dealerships lording it over the *taco de cabeza* stands and hole-in-the-wall bakeries that reminded you it was still Mexico. It was an open, clean town. It was not a town to hide in.

Except today, Kathleen hoped, as her fingers tightened on the steering wheel and the downtown traffic began to squeeze alongside her on the boulevard.

She tried to appear as if in no particular rush as she

approached the *comandancia*. Then, a block before she reached it, she made a squealing, unexpected turn. The same traffic policeman who'd tried to take her plates before looked up and blew his whistle. The police car lost a few precious seconds as it cut off a pickup truck to follow her. Through the tinted glass of its windshield, the men in it were still only silhouettes of heads, faceless.

She steered again for the *zócalo*. Ahead she saw the same speaker on the bandstand, his hands flying as if he were throwing pizza dough. But as she'd hoped, the crowds were even thicker now, and a brass band in purple uniforms was trying to form up in the street. Next to it was a students' group, red banners dipping and sagging. She aimed.

A snake, her mother used to tell her on hikes, always goes for the second person in line. The first one gets his attention; he's ready for the second. Now she had a chance to test that theory.

Over the air conditioner's whoosh, she heard the chants around her, the chants she'd been hearing for days: *Un pueblo unido, jamás será vencido, un pueblo unido, jamás será vencido*, over and over again, like a raucous church litany, *a people united, will never be defeated*. . . .

She unsnapped Luis's seat belt. "Get down," she motioned. "On the floor."

He looked blank. "Now!" she signed to him in their shorthand. His face darkened as if he were about to cry, but he slipped off the seat and made a ball of himself on the carpet.

She swerved toward the band first, so close that a tuba banged off the Ford's front fender. Tall plumed hats toppled as the players scrambled against each other to avoid her. Then she cut the car hard back into the street for a few yards, and made an S curve toward the crowd of students. They'd seen her swipe at the band, and were already scattering. Don't let me hit anyone, let them jump the right way, she prayed as she cut away from the shouts and angry fists that slammed against the side of the car.

She allowed herself a quick glance in the rear-view mirror. The seconds she'd gained turning off the boulevard had been enough. The students and band members swirled behind the Ford like a wake behind a boat; the police car's lights were flashing, its siren was screaming, and it was utterly mired. As she screeched around the corner of the *zócalo*, she saw the students leaping onto the other car, rocking it, tipping it.

On the way back she avoided downtown. She stopped in a neighborhood of low, featureless working people's houses long enough to help Luis back up into the seat and wipe away a glisten of tears on his eyes. She gave him her first genuine smile of the day.

Two

ALICIA DURA'S HOUSE WAS MEXICAN-
blue cinder block, set back behind a picket fence and
shaded by shaggy eucalyptus trees. The street was
pleasant. The houses were small and the yards dusty,
but they were all cooled or separated by eucalyptus
and wispy Sonoran palo verde trees and prickly pear
hedges, or hidden behind tall stands of flowering

oleanders. A girl about Luis's age clattered over the uneven sidewalk on a rickety tricycle, watched by cats pretending to sleep on shady porches, and chased by a pair of puppies who made silly, yipping leaps behind her and tumbled on top of one another. On the street in front of the house, a dented pickup truck was parked, and three old sedans were scattered haphazardly in the yard.

A woman in jeans watched Kathleen's new Ford from a doorway across the street with suspicion as it pulled in behind the pickup. Luis sat up in the seat and looked enviously at the girl on the tricycle. Kathleen understood. For a moment she imagined herself sitting on the porch with the woman, drinking coffee while Luis and the little girl played on the quiet street and waiting for nothing but the drift of afternoon into the cool of evening and a plate of *chili colorado* for dinner and some mindless game show on television and then sleep.

But she looked at her watch. Less than two hours.

The cautious teenaged girl who met her at Alicia Dura's door repeated her name aloud to herself, memorizing it, before she disappeared into the dimness of the house with the message about the blond *gringa* who wanted to see Alicia. Through the sprung, ripped screen Kathleen could hear a rapid Spanish conversation stop abruptly—several voices, both men's and women's. There was nothing about the house to make her afraid, Kathleen thought, only uneasy, as if she'd stumbled into a party to which she hadn't been invited. She squeezed Luis's hand. He squeezed back.

When the girl returned, she held the door for Kathleen. *"Entre, por favor.* Come in, please," she said neutrally.

Past a shadowy, L-shaped entry hall with a collection of old sweaters hung in it, the house opened out into a living room. Two lumpy, blue-plastic couches and a few tattered easy chairs took up most of the room. The empty spaces between them had been filled out with dinette chairs for the dozen or so people in the room. A faded, cheap carpet hid part of the gray-green, ubiquitous Mexican concrete tiles, and the walls held a collection of fly-specked family photographs. Most of the people were *campesinos* who watched Kathleen and Luis silently as the two came in. Her uneasiness increased. She remembered the men at the police *comandancia* and the crowds on the street staring at her. No one got up from his seat.

A woman on the couch who Kathleen thought might match the fuzzy newspaper photographs of Alicia Dura said, "You wanted to see Alicia Dura?"

Kathleen darted her eyes around the room a last time. "Yes."

"You're the wife of Jorge Zaragoza?"

"Yes."

"You've come very late."

"Are you Alicia Dura?"

The woman nodded slightly.

"I'm not here about your letter," Kathleen said.

"So your husband did get it?"

"No. I did—this morning. He hasn't seen it. And it doesn't matter now."

"That's true," Alicia Dura said. "What can I do for you, señora?"

"I have to talk to you. It's important. Please."

Alicia Dura studied Kathleen a moment, her and Luis, who held his mother tightly and seemed to be trying to make sense out of the black-moustached face in one of the photographs on the wall. There was no challenge in Alicia Dura's look, only thoughtfulness. It was the look of a woman who was used to deciding how she *should* feel before she felt. Kathleen's eyes were becoming accustomed to the dim light in the room; even with the midday heat, all the curtains were drawn. She could see Alicia Dura more clearly now. She was a plain woman, somewhere in her middle thirties, with her black hair done in no particular fashion. She was a little overweight, comfortably so, and she wore a plain, cheap skirt and blouse, no stockings, and imitation-leather, sensible shoes. She would be colorless and schoolteacherly, Kathleen thought, except for her face. It was serene and firm, with something at once kind and tough about her eyes that arrested you far more than any kind of dime-novel revolutionary flamboyance. Kathleen remembered that all the pictures she had seen of her always had her in front of a crowd. And every face was turned toward her, every pair of eyes locked on her.

"Then we'll talk," Alicia Dura said at length. She said it efficiently, but not coldly. She turned to the other people in the room and nodded. In a scrape of chairs, they wordlessly got to their feet and began to file out through a door that Kathleen saw led to the kitchen. She heard a screen door to the back patio slap, and the conversation pick up as the first few of the *campesinos* left the house. "Carlos, stay, please," Alicia said to one of the men. Kathleen noticed him for the first time. Standing, he was a head taller than the others. There was no mestizo or Indian in his features: his hair was more auburn than black, and behind his glasses his eyes were a pale green. He was dressed in work khakis, but his body was slim, his face tan but not sunburnt, and his hands those of a man who was more at home holding a book than a plow handle. He sat back down in the chair across from Alicia. She motioned for Kathleen to sit on the couch beside her, but made no attempt to introduce Carlos or explain his presence. Luis clambered up into Kathleen's lap when she sat.

"Your husband was better than most," Alicia said. "Our people could almost live on what he paid. I think he would have been willing to give us title to part of his land and work out something about the machinery. It would have been better that way."

"I didn't know he'd been in touch with you. He's in Mexico City."

"No, you wouldn't have known." Was it pity or sarcasm in the woman's voice? "And, yes, I'm aware he's in Mexico City. I'm sorry he left—I don't think he was a particularly altruistic man, but for his class he was a reasonable one." She reached out and touched Luis's hand. "You can see the family in him. He's the deaf one, isn't he?"

"He is," Kathleen said, defensive.

Alicia smiled. "It's my job to know those things, señora. Don't be surprised."

"Then do you know about this?" Kathleen pulled the letter from her purse and handed it to her.

Alicia read it, then handed it silently over to Carlos. "I'm not likely to have ever gotten one of those," she said.

"But you know about the Game?"

Alicia shrugged. "I've heard of it. Why did you bring that to me?"

Carlos handed the letter back to Kathleen. Was he mute, too, like Luis, Kathleen wondered. He made her nervous, the way a microphone in the room would have. "There's no one else," she said.

"Not your husband?"

"I can't contact him."

"He has friends."

"No. I don't think they're friends. And I've been to the police. I'm sure they're involved, too."

Alicia Dura gave a little "of course" flip with her hand. "I surely don't have that sort of money, señora."

Kathleen took a deep breath. How much did she mean of what she was about to say? But she had to say it. What choice did she have now? "I trust you, Señora Dura. You're probably the only human being I can get to whose motives I think I understand. You might see me as your enemy, but that doesn't matter. If I ask you for something, and you say you'll do it, I think I can believe you."

"What do you know about me, Señora Zaragoza? How much could you possibly know about me?"

"That doesn't matter, either. I have no other chances left to take."

Alicia Dura waved toward a door leading off the room. "In that bedroom fifteen years ago, I saw my father murdered. He was asleep, and gunmen from your friend Enrique Crouse's father came in to do it. I was sitting just where I am now, my mother and I. My father was trying to organize a peasants' union— the one I lead now. They left me alone when I took over for my father because I was a girl then, and they didn't think I could do anything. Now they're too cautious to kill me because I've succeeded, and they don't know which way the wind's blowing. You can tell me that your husband and friends are not like that because they're a different generation. Some may be. But understand this, señora: if some of them thought they could do it quietly, they'd see me dead tonight. And you come into my house and tell me you trust me and ask for my help. Do you know what you're doing? Do you truly know what you're doing?"

"The only thing I can do," Kathleen said. Luis settled in her lap. She felt his smallness against her.

Alicia and Carlos exchanged looks. "Then what do you want?" Alicia said.

Kathleen knew she was rushing her words now, afraid of losing them. "I want to get into my husband's country house."

"Why?"

"I think there's money there."

"Enough for that?" Alicia motioned toward the letter that Kathleen still held.

"I don't know. There might be."

"Dollars."

"Yes."

"Illegal dollars."

"I don't care what kind they are."

"No. And truthfully, I don't either." The dim light cut heavy lines into her face as she glanced again at Carlos as if she were checking something about herself in a mirror. "Señora Zaragoza, forgive me a pointless question. Do you realize how many of my people don't have enough food for their children so that your husband could accumulate that much money?"

"You know I don't. But that's not *my* children's fault, either."

Alicia waved the answer away. "Do you think that because you say you trust me enough to tell me about the money that I'm obligated to let you get to it—is that it? That I'll let my own people go hungry—no matter how truly sorry I may be for your children, or how much I might detest this 'game' that's chosen you? You don't look like a stupid woman, señora. Don't insult me by thinking I am."

"I don't think that. I'm offering you a trade."

The uncertain pity that had been in Alicia's voice was on her face now. "It would have to be a very large trade, señora."

"My husband won't contest your land takeover. And the machinery—the tractors, the combines, everything—will go back onto the land. How many years would it take this government's bureaucracy to give you that? How many people would go hungry while you wait?''

Alicia's expression didn't change, didn't give Kathleen a clue to an opening for hope.

"You can make a commune out of it, sell the machinery, give it away—I don't care. The money's nothing compared to all of that, is it?'' She wanted to plead with this woman—beg, if she had to. But not now. Now was for bargaining, convincing.

From Kathleen's left, Carlos's voice interrupted. It was deep, quiet, and there was a trace of unidentifiable accent in it. "The land is your husband's, señora.''

"My children are his, too.''

"People in desperate situations make desperate bargains,'' he said. "Later they sometimes change their minds. I have no doubt your husband would agree—today.''

She willed herself to face him, expecting to find hate, hardness in his face that would steel her, would let her hate him back. But he was looking at her only in the way she imagined he might study a problem on a blackboard. "And tomorrow,'' she said. "He'll keep his word tomorrow.''

"Señora . . .''

"Because you'll have my son.''

"I beg your pardon?'' Alicia said.

Kathleen closed her eyes a moment, to shut out even this weak light. "You won't have to trust me—or my husband. You'll have my son. You'll have Luis.''

"I don't understand you, señora,'' Alicia said.

"I want you to take Luis, hide him somewhere with your people until all this is over."

Alicia blinked. "You're proposing that seriously?"

"Where else can he be safe? And how else can you trust me?"

The expression on Alicia's face slowly changed to one Kathleen thought might have approached a kind of appreciation, a kind of recognition of something between them for the first time. "I see," she said.

A silence broken only by the voices of the *campesinos* in the patio outside held the room for a long moment. Even Luis seemed to feel it, and wiggled uncomfortably in Kathleen's lap. She stroked his arm to calm him—and herself.

Carlos spoke first, his voice still quiet. "It's more danger for your people, Alicia."

"It is, yes."

"And if her husband decides to claim we've kidnapped the boy? What position would that put us in with the government?"

"You'll have our child!" Kathleen broke in, her own voice rising in anger, just as it had when Enrique was explaining the insane rules of the Game to her. There had to be someone, someone here who could see one clean, obvious line of reasoning! "If I wanted to put him in *more* danger, would I be here? Would I be giving him to you? And who are you?" she said to Carlos. "What do you have to do with this?"

"He's an adviser," Alicia said, soothing her. "Just an adviser." Carlos didn't react. "But I listen to him."

"He doesn't know my husband. You do. Would Jorge *use* his children?"

"Who can say that, señora?"

"I can. *I* can say it."

Alicia paused, then nodded—more to herself than to anyone in the room, as if she were confirming something to herself. "Understand me," she said. "I have no idea how much you know about how we operate. I don't make decisions alone." She gestured toward the voices on the back patio. "We discuss things first and reach a consensus."

"There's no *time* . . ."

"I know that. So I want you to realize that most everything I've ever worked for is at risk in the decision I'm going to make. Unless you do exactly as you say you will, and do it in only a matter of days, I'll know you've lied to me. You're trading for time now, Señora Zaragoza, just that. And you have no room to argue; whatever your risk, it's no less than mine, and it's the least risk you have now. *Comprende?*"

Don't hesitate, Kathleen told herself. The shadow is there, is still cast by this red light, is not going to vanish. Not yet, not yet. "I understand," she said. She pulled Luis more tightly to her.

"And I can't be responsible for what I can't foresee while we have him. My people come first. They'll take care of him well, but they'll come first if anything goes wrong anywhere."

"Yes."

Alicia nodded again, once more efficient and moving.

"Carlos, take her in the truck. I'll tell the people in the patio after you've gone."

"They won't be pleased," Carlos said.

"No. But then they can decide what to do with me, can't they?" She got to her feet.

Kathleen held Luis tightly for a moment more, so tightly she was afraid she would frighten him if she didn't let go. He raised his face to her, and she signed to him as briefly as she could that she had to go for a while, but that he would stay with the lady.

"Can I play with the girl on the tricycle?" he signed.

Kathleen asked Alicia Dura. "On the patio," Alicia said. "I think it can be arranged." She took Luis's hand.

"He's probably hungry," Kathleen blurted. "And he's really fine about making himself understood. He's good-natured. He's a good child." Her voice broke, and she stopped herself.

"I know," Alicia Dura said, and glanced at a clock on an end table. "She has barely an hour and a half, Carlos."

"*Sí.*" He went to the door and waited for Kathleen to go out ahead of him. Even in his movements there was a quietness—nothing like meekness, only a quietness. "You should leave your car keys," he said. "I think they'll want to move your car."

Kathleen found her keys in her purse and dropped them onto the table beside the clock. Even that unlikely escape was now gone. She looked at Luis from the doorway. He was trying to see through a crack in the curtains. She knew he was looking for the girl on the tricycle.

Neither she nor Carlos spoke on the way out of town. The streets were fuller now, and through the open windows of the pickup she heard the bands practicing for the parade. The air that rushed in the windows was hot as air from a hair dryer. As soon as it dried the sweat that made loose wisps of hair cling to her neck, it brought new sweat. But the hot wind felt good to her because it kept the chill inside her a little deeper and kept her from trembling.

She tried to keep the image of Luis close to her. Her two older children seemed to her to be in a book somewhere now, the same book her life had come from before Mexico. And it was a safe book. Nothing could happen to them in it. But Luis was here, and she'd given him up. So she had to hold on to every piece of him that she could.

Almost from the beginning he'd had more of her thoughts than the other boys. Not that she loved him more, she believed, but that he had needed her more. From his first year, she and Jorge had known something was wrong with him. Half a dozen different doctors had diagnosed half a dozen different things, from hyperactivity to "motor skill problems," as if they were as reluctant to admit the truth as she and Jorge had been. But the two of them had accepted the right diagnosis when it came at last—she thanked

God for that—and in Luis's second year they'd started to work with him. They had learned sign language along with him, and had even taught Guadalupe enough to say most things she wanted to him. They'd joked that he was lucky—the sign for most things was the same in English and in Spanish, so he was automatically bilingual.

But now he was learning to speech read—to lipread, Kathleen had been taught to call it when she was a girl. And next year or the year after he would have to go to Tucson, to the school for the deaf. One doctor had told her he should have gone already. But he was only six! She couldn't bear to let him go yet. When he was seven maybe, or eight at the most. And not to a school in Boston or New York. Those were too far from her. That was her latest compromise, a selfish one she'd learned to live with. And one that Jorge had understood, too, as he had understood so many things she was grateful to him for. And loved him for.

If she had let Luis go, she thought, he'd be in Tucson now.

Stop it, Kathleen Ballance, Kathleen Zaragoza, she told herself. You'll sound like a soap opera. Then she turned her face toward the hot air from the window so this man beside her, this Carlos whoever-he-was, wouldn't see her crying.

They were leaving the outskirts of Obregón now. The limitless, flat fields stretched off in all directions through a haze of heat and dust to the raw, dry desert mountains in the distance. Only in a few of the fields were people at work. Whether they were fields still not invaded, or ones the new owners were working, she couldn't tell. The people on the land looked the same, were the same, no matter who owned it.

Carlos was the first to break the silence. "You don't have to hide your crying," he said.

She felt invaded, like the lands. "It's not your concern."

"All right," he said, his tone not changing. "It's not."

They rode in silence awhile more, and Kathleen realized in the silence that a voice, any voice, had been better than nothing but the sound of the dry wind through the window. She couldn't say she particularly liked this man, but she liked his voice, liked the calm of it. That didn't make much sense, she knew. But she'd take what she could get.

"You have an accent," she said.

"So do you."

"Of course I do. I wasn't born in Mexico."

"I was."

"Where?"

"In Puebla."

"That's not your accent. People from Puebla don't have one."

"I've lived other places. For a long time." He kept his eyes on the road.

"Then you've picked up an accent."

"Okay."

They rode some more. "All right," she said finally. "I give up. Where did you live?"

"Lots of places."

"Mainly?"

"Havana, mainly."

"What were you doing there?" She was shocked, as she supposed he'd expected she would be, but kept her voice even.

"In schools. Learning things."

"And what are you doing here?"

"Advising. Alicia told you. She and her people make all the decisions."

"Are you a communist?" Stupid or not, she wanted to know—to know anything that might make a difference.

He shrugged.

"Where else did you live?"

"San Francisco for a while."

"Then you know the United States?"

"Some of it."

It was a straw, and she grasped it. She wanted, needed, some kind of bond between herself and this man on whom she was utterly dependent for the next hour. Maybe the most important hour of her life. "Which did you like better—Havana or San Francisco?" she asked in English.

"It's a trade-off. The climate's better in Havana," he answered in Spanish. He wasn't taking the bait. He wouldn't give her the language advantage.

"That's not what I meant."

"It's still a trade-off. But I stayed in Havana longer."

"Did they send you here—the Cubans?"

He turned to her. "Look. Mexico's not Cuba. What

73

works there won't work here, not all of it. Some of it will. I'm trying to find out what will."

"And taking my husband's land works."

"Probably," he said, and turned back to the road. "I'm sorry for what's happening to you. That letter's a goddamned vicious thing. All of this shouldn't happen to you at once."

"No," she said. "It shouldn't."

She recognized things along the road: stands of mesquite, washes, lean-to sheds that advertised honey or vegetables or tacos, or that seemed held together by the rusting Coca-Cola or Seven-Up signs nailed against their sides. They were getting close to the turnoff now. The familiarity of things brought back too much, hurt too much. Jorge loved this land, and she loved it through him. She looked away from the landscape toward Carlos. His glasses sat naturally on him, and beneath them his face was strong. It seemed to echo his movements—quiet, but not meek. He was a handsome man, she let herself realize for the first time. She guessed his people as European or American no more than a generation back.

"Do you have another name?" she asked him.

"Only the one I was born with." He smiled.

"You know that's not what I mean, either."

"Just Carlos. For now."

"What will happen to my son?"

"You said you trusted Alicia. So do I—to keep her word, either way."

Whatever warmth she'd started to feel for him blew away, froze. She moved her eyes away from him to the electric-blue plastic Virgin that twisted from the rear-view mirror in the wind.

"We're here," he said. The pickup slowed and bumped across a cattle guard onto the dirt road that led to the country house. She didn't answer him. With a pang, she saw the etched wooden sign, ZARAGOZA, still in place beside the road.

The country house sat about three-quarters of a mile off the highway. Kathleen tried to keep her remembered picture of it intact as long as she could before reality ripped it up: the shady, white-washed adobe of the old part, the comfortable wooden angles and screened porches of the newer section, the way the shadows of pines and cottonwoods had played over it all when she and Jorge were first married and had time for cool, white-wine weekends there. Then the children's voices from the old-tire swing Jorge had hung for them in a cottonwood. . . . Suddenly the peacocks, the antique furniture—all the things she had always believed didn't really mean anything to her—became terribly important. She wanted them to all still be there, wanted it to be yesterday, to be last year again. But she brought herself up sharply as they rounded a patch of creosote bushes, and she saw that one of the phalanx of Italian cypresses Jorge's father had planted as a windbreak years ago was gone, like a missing tooth. Or no, it wasn't gone: it was stripped of its branches and laid across the road. A roadblock, she thought, and the very sound of the word in her mind tightened her fear.

The pickup bumped to a stop a yard from the

roadblock. Through the neat rows of the orchards that surrounded the house, Kathleen could make out the glint of the sun reflected from the windows. She was surprised to realize she was almost shocked that the house was still there. Somehow she supposed she had thought it, too, had disappeared like the peacocks and the water in the swimming pool.

The doors to a panel truck parked in the cypress shade beside the roadblock swung open, and a man and a woman stepped down to the ground. Half a dozen other people stood up from among bushes at the base of the cypresses. Some of them carried heavy sticks, like clubs.

Carlos beeped the horn and waved as he got out of the pickup. The couple from the cab of the panel truck beamed when they saw him, and waved back. Kathleen heard loud, twangy *ranchero* music blaring from the truck, even at the fifty or so yards' distance.

That wasn't the way it would have happened in the movies, she thought—no *ranchero* guitars and concertinas, only militant marches. Nor would the chubby man in Levi's who shook Carlos's hand be wearing a Caterpillar baseball hat. Nor the woman with him have her hair up in curlers, or be wearing a T-shirt that claimed, in English, I ♥ Los Angeles. Nor would the others who crowded around him be dressed in Lee overalls or denim jackets with U.S. Marine Corps emblems on them, or be trailing the earphones of Walkman radios. She hadn't expected that; from the pictures in the newspapers Jorge subscribed to, she'd expected fatigue uniforms and raised fists and angry strangers' faces. But behind these smiles, she even recognized some of the faces as belonging to people who'd worked on Jorge's land, this land. And it was a fair for them, a fiesta day.

"Señora Zaragoza," Carlos said, breaking away from the group of *campesinos* and bringing the couple from the panel truck with him. "I want to present your hosts to you. Juan and Miranda Diaz, cochairmen of the Armando Dura Collective."

"Which is this land, I take it," she said.

"Formerly it was called something else, I imagine," he said. "It's named after Alicia's father now." He spoke with his usual calm seriousness, but Kathleen saw in his eyes he was enjoying himself. All right, let him, she thought. In his place, she might, too. She didn't care if they all stood at attention and sang the "Internationale" in Ukrainian, as long as they moved that log and let her through. In the old pickup the trip had taken half an hour. A half an hour back, and she had twenty-five minutes. And what would it take to get the strongbox open without a key?

Awkward, embarrassed, Juan and Miranda, Caterpillar cap and curlers, held out their hands.

It was clear they had been coming onto the property for days before the invasion became "official" and Ramón had gathered the courage to tell her about it. The pool was almost empty, yes: Ramón had apparently cut the water off early, and the people in the corrugated-tin and straw lean-tos had been drinking, bathing, and washing with what they could salvage. And the orchards were stripped. Even though some of the fruit hadn't been ready yet—the grapefruit, the oranges—it had been eaten. Kathleen's first reaction was anger. The orchards had been her special care— there was something about the order of the rows, the cool shade between them, the fragrances, the dependable progress of the trees from flower to fruit each year that comforted her. What damned right did these people have to touch *her* orchards, to ruin a whole year's cycle?

And then she thought, what else did they have to eat? She endured their silent stares as they sat on makeshift stools, or stood slack armed in front of their lean-tos and watched her. Most of them didn't know her, but they recognized her. And yet they only stared. Why didn't they shout at her or throw stones?

She knew it was because this was Mexico, this country whose patience was as long and terrible as the revolutions that came when the patience finally ended. The presence of these people on her and Jorge's lands told her that the patience was burned down, was guttering like a spent candle.

"Why didn't you turn the water back on?" she asked Juan as they approached the main house.

He adjusted his Caterpillar cap, still embarrassed to have to speak to her. "Because your man, Ramón, smashed the pumps, señora."

She walked ahead. She wanted to get the money and be gone from here as quickly as possible.

Carlos and Juan and two other men moved the

washstand in the kitchen. It was all there as Guadalupe had said: the paving stone, and beneath that the iron lid, its black paint flaking and rust spots showing through. You could still see where the pipe had been dug up beside it years ago.

"No key?" Carlos asked.

Kathleen shook her head.

"Best to leave the lid alone," Carlos said. "Smash the concrete."

While one of the men went for a spade and sledge-hammers, Kathleen looked around her. A family was camped here in the kitchen—a naked boy about Luis's age watched her from a pallet against the wall. Through the door into the dining room, she saw that at least two other families had set up there. One was apparently using the dining room table—part of the furniture from Spain—as a bed. None of the other furniture seemed to have been used. Guadalupe would be pleased to hear that, she thought. What she wouldn't be pleased to hear was that there had been camp fires on the tiles of the dining room floor, fires that had left huge smudges on the whitewashed adobe ceiling. The house smelled of wood smoke now, wood smoke and tomato sauce and chili peppers and diapers. It was no longer her and Jorge's house, no longer a place where she belonged. It was like the line from that Lorca poem she'd read in school: "My house is no longer my house, and I am no longer I. . . ." Was it true, this quickly? All those years and memories flushed away so easily?

She checked her watch. Fifteen minutes. "Hurry them," she said to Carlos. He nodded.

The dirt came up quickly. But even though the concrete had been underground for probably seventy years, it was still thick and hard. First they tried sledgehammers alone, then when those failed, they used chisels to start cracks.

It took five minutes to get the first crack, three for the second. In ten minutes there was a network of them.

"Use the sledgehammers alone now," Carlos told the two *campesinos* who were doing most of the work. A crowd had gathered outside the windows and doors, marveling and hazarding guesses as to what the amazing box might hold, that such important people should be spending so much energy on it.

With the first two blows of the sledgehammers, a chunk fell out of the concrete. Then other chunks, until one of them toppled inward into the box. Half a dozen more blows, Kathleen knew, and there would be room for a hand to get inside. The two men swung furiously.

And then they stopped. The yells of the women outside the windows rose above the thunks of the sledgehammers. The men, listening, held their hammers poised.

Carlos went to the window first, then Kathleen was beside him. Women scooped small children from the lean-tos and shouted for older ones to follow them as they ran for the fields. Men frantically gathered up sticks, pieces of pipe, and hoe handles that they'd laid by. Juan and Miranda shoved through the people at the door, already giving orders. Beyond them, in the fields to the north, cornstalks and beanpoles parted like waters as half a dozen pickups and four-by-fours slalomed out into the clear toward the house, their engines howling as they fought for traction in the loose soil.

"Who are they?" Kathleen shouted to Carlos over the chaos.

"State police? Your husband's gunmen? You tell me!" he shouted back.

"I swear to you . . ." she began.

"Get into the fields, then, if you don't have an appointment with them."

"The money!"

"Too late."

He was past her so quickly she had no chance to answer. Outside, the first of the pickups slid to a stop. Men piled out of it with hoses and billy sticks; rifles lowered themselves from the windows of the cab. A wave of *campesinos* met the men from the truck, swinging, flailing with whatever they had. A rifle went off—into the air, Kathleen saw with relief. More trucks and four-by-fours stopped. More men, most of their eyes hidden behind mirrored sunglasses, leapt out. Into the air, Kathleen thought, for the moment. And then?

She snatched a shovel from against the wall. The noise outside grew louder as she pitched and shoveled the dirt back into the hole until enough of it was gone for her to scatter the rest with a broom. Then, to get the paving stone back in place, she had to make a wedge of herself, her back against a kitchen counter and feet shoving the heavy square of slate until it thudded into place. She was biting off hunks of the dry air by the time she threw her shoulder against the mahogany washstand, put all her strength into it, and knew it wouldn't move.

It didn't matter now. A glance through the window told her she had to go, to get away somewhere. Two men lay sprawled on the ground, blood puddling beside one of them. Another was being dragged by his hair toward a pickup. And three of the men with mirrored sunglasses were battling their way toward the house, only yards away.

She ran through the dining room, through Jorge's office, into the living room. But it was no good there, either. Even if she made it out the front door, she'd step into the same small war that was going on outside the kitchen.

This part of the house was the newer section. The kitchen and dining room were the original small adobe house Jorge's great-grandfather had lived in when he was clearing the land. But this part Jorge's grandfather had added. It was wooden, with a warren of bedrooms and closets and baths for the children and grandchildren who had crowded in through the years. It was a warren she was sure the men outside would search when they fought their way inside. Where could she hide?—not outside, not inside.

She now heard footsteps, shouts, from the kitchen. With no clear purpose, she took the stairs to the second floor two at a time. But if they searched the downstairs, they would search the upstairs, too, and even slipping out a window was impossible here. She ran from one bedroom door to the next, opening and closing, opening and closing, hoping to find some escape she knew wasn't there.

At the end of the long upstairs corridor, she saw through the window that some of the lean-tos in the yard were burning. In the distance, she could make out scattering figures breaking trails through the fields. The panel truck that had been parked at the road-block was gone, and beyond the cypresses she saw a rooster tail of dust marking its progress toward the highway. She ran her eyes across the yard, trying to find Carlos's tall form in all the motion. She couldn't. Had he been the one in the panel truck—or was he just out of her vision, swinging sticks like the others, like people just out of the jungles?

The voices seemed closer now, at the foot of the stairs.

Stairs. There had been stairs, more stairs. Jorge had showed her once—here, at the end of the corridor, more stairs that led up to a widow's walk his grandfather had put on the flat peak of the roof in some fit of fancy. The stairs had given way to the need for another bathroom, but you could still get up there, Jorge had told her. A ceiling panel in the new bathroom, she remembered as she threw open the door. There! Above the washbasin!

A step onto the unflushed toilet, then onto the washbasin and she could reach the low ceiling. She pushed the plasterboard panel. It scraped, snowed plaster dust, and moved!

Her free hand just reached the bottom rung of a wooden ladder nailed against the wall above the panel. She grabbed it, then let the panel drop back down and rest against the back of her hand while she eased her other hand into position. Then, working her head up past the panel like a cat through a cat door, she pulled herself high enough to get a purchase on the medicine cabinet with her foot. She let go with one hand now, and reached the next rung. Then the next, and the next, until her whole body was inside the vertical tunnel to the roof. Spiderwebs brushed her as she eased the panel back into place with her foot and let the darkness, the hot closeness hide her.

Her fingers found a trapdoor above her. She knew she might well be best hidden here in this tunnel. But no, she couldn't do it, not stay in this upright coffin. She fumbled around the edges of the trapdoor until she found a latch. The strength almost gone from her fingers, she jerked at the ring of the old-fashioned spring-loaded latch. Pain shot through her fingers. The latch didn't budge. She balanced herself better and jerked again. And this time it snapped sharply back and a crack of sunlight appeared around the trapdoor.

When her hand touched the hot tar paper of the roof it was as if she'd touched the burner on a stove. She snatched it back. Sun flooded into the tunnel, and seemed to carry the shouts from outside with it.

She tried to picture the roof, to imagine a place there might be shade.

Chimneys, she thought. There were chimneys, two of them. They always had been the first things her eyes had picked out as she approached the house in the first years she and Jorge had been married, before the cypresses grew tall enough to hide them. She lifted her head through the trapdoor. The sun was barely past midpoint. Yet enough, she prayed, enough to make a few inches of shade. She flung the trapdoor fully open, heaved her body as high as it would go on the ladder, slapped her hand hard onto the roof to mask the pain of the burning, and tumbled herself onto the roof.

She kept low so she couldn't be seen from the ground. At the first chimney, she found no more than a foot and a half of shadow. But it was enough. She pressed her back against the chimney and slid down it, the rough bricks feeling good through Jorge's work shirt. Her sandaled feet stuck out into the sun, no matter how closely she tried to pull her legs to herself. Dear God, she thought, I'm worrying about sunburn.

She tried to focus on the face of her watch, but couldn't. The heat, her fatigue, the fact she hadn't really eaten since last night, all seemed to be conspiring against a simple thing like focusing her eyes. She closed them. Just to clear them, to rest them a moment. Then she tried to open them again, but the brightness from the sun on the roof pressed against them like hands, and she couldn't.

*   *   *

The silence woke her. She heard a fly buzzing around her face, heard a breeze skittering a leaf across the roof beside her, but nothing more. And when she opened her eyes, she saw that her feet were no longer in the sun.

She rubbed her eyes with her fingertips and felt sweat burn in them. She still had to close one to focus, but she forced the hands of her watch to make sense at last. They read two o'clock.

She stumbled to her feet. At the rotting railing around the widow's walk, she scanned the grounds. From a few of the lean-tos, flames still rose. From others, only smoke. All the pickups, the four-by-fours were gone. Only the old pickup she and Carlos had come in still waited by the pool. Nothing moved except the tall cypresses in the breeze: even the two men she'd seen lying on the ground were gone. It was like an engraving of a scene after a battle in an old book, one from which the artist had decided to remove all the people to make it seem even more desolate.

Her strength had come back slightly—not to normal, but enough to allow her to raise the trapdoor and climb down the ladder without being afraid she would black out again. And as her strength came back, her mind raced ahead. Two o'clock. Even if the money were still there, it would be two-thirty—no, two forty-five counting the time it would take her to dig it out again, if she could—before she got home. Would the man from the Game Committee have waited? Was that against his stinking rules, too?

And Luis. What news had whoever was in the panel truck carried back to Alicia Dura?—that Kathleen had arranged a raid, or that her husband had? That the bargain she'd struck was off? Carlos's first thought had been that she'd been involved on the side of the landowners somehow. But why on earth would she have been? Surely Alicia Dura would see that her only care was for Luis, not for the land. What would a raid like this have gained her? Yet, how else to explain the raid? If the raiders had been state policemen, Jorge *could* have had a hand in it, could have arranged it in one of his meetings with those senators. And if not Jorge, then who? And why now?

God, if she could only *talk* to Jorge, say a dozen words to him, hear his voice . . .

Alicia would keep her word, either way, Carlos had said. The Game Committee never changes its rules, Enrique had said. Kathleen half slid, half ran down the stairs to the first floor. No, she promised herself, no! She wouldn't *let* it be that absolute.

The washstand stood where she'd left it in the kitchen. And the paving stone was still in its place! She'd been sure that the washstand there alone in the middle of the kitchen would call attention to itself, would make one of the men with the mirrored sunglasses sufficiently suspicious to look at the room closely enough to see the fresh dirt, the paving stone with the cement missing from around it. But how could it, she realized now. Everything in the house was moved, shoved aside to make room for pallets and cooking fires. Only she would see the washstand as odd, the dirt out of place. Only she knew the house as it had been. She silently thanked the *campesinos* for their disorder.

She pried the stone up with a chisel. One of the families had left behind a warm Coke, and she drank it. The caffeine and the sugar helped, and after she'd shoveled the loose dirt away, a little of her strength still remained.

The sledgehammer was different, though. She could swing it two, sometimes three times, then would have to rest. What had seemed so near to being done when the two *campesinos* were working took nearly a quarter of an hour alone. But when she put her hand inside the safe and felt the rough texture of a suitcase, she went back to the hammer with new force. In five more minutes the hole in the side of the box had grown large enough for her to slide the suitcase out.

It was a small shock to find it was a piece from the old powder-blue American Tourister set she'd had when she married—and it was oddly comforting, too, as if Jorge had left it for her on purpose. It wasn't locked. And when she opened it, she discovered that as neatly as he packed his clothes for business trips, Jorge had left the hundred-dollar bills counted, tied, and labeled. And a slip of paper with the packets already totaled: $286,540, the slip read, and it was dated two days before he left. Dear God.

She closed her suitcase. It was two twenty-five, her watch said. She thought she remembered Carlos had left the keys in the pickup. Since the men with the mirrored sunglasses hadn't thought the old truck worth driving away, had they thought it even worth checking?

She carried the suitcase from the house as she'd carried weekend bags from it how many hundreds of times before? But this time she didn't look back to make sure everything was closed up and in order.

The keys were in the truck. "Please, God," she said aloud as she slipped behind the wheel. "This once, just this once, let it make sense. Let their rules wait, let everybody's."

Olive-drab Mexican army troops, green *federales*, brown-and-tan state patrolmen, white-over-blue marines, walls of them along Boulevard Juarez, holding back the chanting crowds and flag-waving spectators. Fancy-stepping bands. Workers' groups, student groups with the banners that stretched from curb to curb and their slogans and songs. The dun faithful from the government party, the PRI, shuffling along with their own limp banners and worn exhortations. Uniformed school children, nuns and priests, politicians, little boys in soldier and sailor suits, little girls in folk costumes, Indians in pantaloons and ponchos. Fireworks, exploding like all those people might, Kathleen thought. Like she might, if she couldn't find a way around them.

She was three blocks from home. And home had to be first, her meeting with her "representative" there. The choice had been agony as she drove toward town:

to go first to Alicia Dura's and try to make her see that she was keeping her part of the bargain, or to go home on the desperate hope that Espinoza, the man from the Game Committee, might still be waiting. Everything in her wanted to find Luis, to know that he was safe. But it was no choice. She had two other children, too. She had a husband. Alicia Dura had only one of the people she loved most on earth. The Game Committee had them all.

Maybe because she knew the road better than Carlos, she'd been able to get the pickup to bring her here in a little over twenty minutes. And now this, the parade that stretched as far down Juarez ahead of her as she could see. If she backed up and somehow forced her way through the traffic that had built behind her, she could circle around the reservoir and come over the rutted back road that would take her home. But how long would that take, if she could do it at all? She swung the pickup to the curb and had the key out before the engine had sputtered to a stop.

A string of fireworks went off at her feet as she shoved her way into the crowd with the heavy suitcase. Her shirt was plastered to her, her jeans were filthy, and her hair hung like vines. With luck, she thought, people would take her for drunk or crazy and let her pass. No one would suspect that the battered suitcase she was carrying had over a quarter of a million dollars in it.

The suitcase was a ram. She kept her eyes straight ahead and refused to look at the people who cursed her as she slammed it into their knees. Yet even with the suitcase, getting through the tight carpet of people was as slow as trying to get through drifts of Vermont snow. Already it was after three, and each slow step took an hour, a week. Once a state patrolman motioned for her to stay put, but she ducked down and kept going.

Except for the parked cars with people sitting on roof blankets to get a better view, her own street was mercifully clear—clear, that was, except for the tan police car that had found its way home like a lost cat, and for the newer, unmarked Plymouth with government license plates nuzzling in behind it.

She took in her breath and stepped into a clump of oleanders. The state car could be nothing, some official who wanted to park near the parade route, a cousin of one of her neighbors—anything, even her "representative." But she could still make out the shapes of two men in the police car, and that was what mattered now. She would have to get into the house somehow without those shapes knowing it.

She took the alley behind the Gurrolas' house and said a prayer to whatever canine gods there were that their yippy black dog was asleep for once. Then she cut through the easement beside the Cuadras' house and came out midway down the block in front of her own house. The police car, parked on the other side of the house, was out of sight.

Curiously, she thought, she wasn't as afraid as she thought she would be. She dug in the geranium pot by the front door for the hidden key and knew that some things had already been decided. Either the "representative" had waited, and the Game Committee would take the money and abide by its rules, or the "representative" was gone and her next step was clear: go to Alicia Dura. But for this moment, there was nothing left to fear.

She eased the door open, then clicked it softly behind her. The air conditioning hissed at her and enveloped her. Her breath caught when she heard the low sound of a man's voice somewhere in the house. He was here! He had waited.

As silently as possible, she moved through the living room and into the dining room. If he was waiting, surely he should be in this part of the house. Had Guadalupe made friends with him, as she did everybody, and given him the grand tour? Possibly. But as a precaution, she slipped first into the kitchen and slid the suitcase beneath a counter by the garage door. Then she made a show of opening the door to the garage and closing it loudly. As she started down the hall toward her bedroom, she no longer heard the man's voice.

The first thing that told her something was wrong was the shoe in the hallway. Guadalupe's plastic shoe, abandoned on its side. Guadalupe would let her hands be cut off before she would leave a shoe of hers like that. Kathleen stopped. She listened for the voice again. It didn't come. Ahead of her was her silent bedroom. On either side were the children's rooms, just as silent. She took a step backward.

She was inches from Luis's bedroom door when it swung open. She made a sound in her throat and froze. The tall sergeant in the tailored uniform from the police *comandancia* stood in the door and held her with his eyes.

"Comandante," he said into the silence. "It's her."

Comandante Aguilar, captain's insignia catching the hall light, thin moustache straight as rifles, stepped out of her bedroom. He nodded slightly to her, a progressive man's version of a bow. "I'm relieved to see you, señora," he said.

She found her voice. "Why are you here? Why are you in my house?"

"You came to me this morning, no?"

"And you sent me away."

"I had more information to gather, you recall."

"That doesn't tell me why you've waited for me."

"I'm very sorry, señora. Perhaps this will." He stepped aside for her to come into her bedroom.

Guadalupe's legs, spread as if she were falling from a great height, were all that showed of her from behind Kathleen's bed. One of her shoes was missing. On impulse, Kathleen said her name and started toward her. Aguilar took her arm and held her back.

"No further, señora. Please." He pointed to the bed. On it, resting on a stained pillowcase, lay a heavy ironwood carving of a pelican that Kathleen had brought back from her last trip to the Seri Indian country. Guadalupe had always hated dusting the useless thing. The sharp point of its beak was stained like the pillowcase. "It was not done gently."

*   *   *

She knew that she sat on the couch in the living room and cried, stupidly thinking Guadalupe would be upset if her dirty jeans left smudges, and that the tailored sergeant had said things he might have intended to comfort her. And that Aguilar paced, impatient to get on with what he had to do but too civilized to push. And that she heard the grandfather clock strike three-thirty before he judged her calm enough to talk.

"I asked you to remain here, Señora Zaragoza," he began. "God is wiser than I am. If you had been here, I don't think we would be talking now."

"Why did they want Guadalupe?" she said, and knew she could begin crying again but wouldn't. To grieve was to stop, to give her attention to something that would only lead to greater grieving. But she had to know what she could, to get what she could out of this pompous man before she went on. "What was there in those 'rules' about Guadalupe?"

"Nothing, señora. No one was here from the Game Committee today."

"You know that? You're sure of it?" Somehow she wanted him to be wrong, wanted one thing she thought she knew to be true!

"I'm certain of it. No letter was written to your husband from the Committee."

"Then who did write it?"

"I don't know. It's being investigated."

"Investigated by who?"

"By myself. And by others."

"The Game Committee?"

"By others, señora. Please."

Her anger flashed again. *Others!* "If you knew the letter didn't come from your 'committee,' then why weren't you here? Why didn't you do anything to stop this?"

He dropped his eyes as if she'd slapped him. "We were here a few minutes past two. That was too late."

"You mean you were late? You simply got here late?"

"I had to wait for my information, señora. The streets were bad, as you know. These things take time."

These things take time! Had he really given her that bad line from a Peter Lorre movie and expected it to explain everything? Oh, Mexico, she thought. Oh, dear Jesus. "What about those men outside?"

"They were detained, you recall." He met her eyes again, with a small look of triumph. "You were there, I believe."

"Whoever was here, Comandante, whoever he was representing—why did he have to do that to Guadalupe?" Let him have as many triumphs as he wanted, as long as he had answers—or guesses.

He shrugged. "She recognized someone? Frankly, señora, I don't know yet."

"Then the letter—do you have any idea at all who could have sent it?"

"I've considered it, Señora Zaragoza. Someone in your family? I don't think so. A close friend who would know about your family? They would surely all

95

know that your husband is away—and besides, who of *your* friends would need to do something like that? I know of only one other group who has had reason to gather detailed information on your family. One other organization who has no place else to turn for money and needs it desperately. I think you follow me, no?"

There was no more possibility of tears, no more thought of them. She felt stunned, felt that she was the one the heavy carving had come down on. She started to speak, couldn't, then began again. Aguilar waited, his face as stiff as the carving's. "Will you go with me to her?" she said.

"I explained to you, señora. I'm sorry, but it's politically impossible now."

"Then what *will* you do?"

"Wait. The right time will come."

Wait? Now? The bastard! Kathleen got to her feet. "You'll have to excuse me," she said.

Aguilar gave her a questioning look.

"The bathroom. I've got to go to the bathroom. With your permission."

He nodded. She brushed past him into the dining room. "Señora Zaragoza?" he said. She stopped, her back still to him. "Where is your son, señora?"

"With a friend." If she told him the truth, what good would it do her? It would only add one more person to those who knew where Luis was. Don't trust the police, Jorge had told her. Yes, she thought. Yes, I'm listening now. She turned to Aguilar. "Have you tried to contact my husband, Comandante?"

"Yes. I've asked our people in Mexico City to help. He *is* staying at the Maria Isabel with the others, no?"

"Yes. Will you keep trying?"

"You're very welcome to try for yourself, señora. From the *comandancia*. We're there to serve you."

Hypocritical ass, she thought. "Then tell me something. Did any of your people—or the state's—raid the *campesinos* at my country house today?"

"Not to my knowledge. Why would we?"

"You know there was a raid?"

"I do."

"Then who did it?"

"It's being investigated."

"Oh," she said, and started to turn away.

"I take it you were there, señora?"

If nothing else did, her clothing, her hair would tell him if she lied. "Yes."

"Were you successful?"

"In what, Comandante?"

"You were looking for something there."

"I didn't find it." God, how he'd like to get his hands on that, she knew.

"I see."

In the hallway, she veered away toward the kitchen. She stopped at the guest bathroom off the kitchen a moment, opened the door, then closed it for the noise. In the kitchen, she slid open as quietly as possible the drawer that held the spare keys. Then, her heart almost stopping when the magnetic catch on the cabinet door clicked, she took the suitcase. With a stealth she hadn't used since she'd come in late from dates in high school, she opened the garage door, went out, then locked the deadbolt behind her with a key. She put the suitcase in the cab of Jorge's pickup, then the key in the ignition before she went to press the button to raise the garage door. By the time it rattled up, she had the engine of the pickup racing. She heard the antenna twang against the not yet fully open door as she backed into the street. And as she turned the corner, she caught only a quick glimpse of the comandante and the sergeant running from her house's front door and waving frantically to the puzzled, uncomprehending men who were leaping from the police cruiser.

Her first thought as she raced toward the back road that would take her around the parade was how miserably convenient Guadalupe's death must be for Aguilar. He had the perfect weapon dropped into his lap. It was a gift, no matter which direction the winds blew. He could blame Alicia Dura for something he may have done himself, if the government backed down from Jorge's committee. Or if the government kept on supporting the *campesinos*, he could find somebody else more convenient on whom to blame poor Guadalupe's death—or find nobody at all, if that suited him better. All ways, he could please the winning side. And again, in an even more direct and terrible way, Kathleen knew her own lifeboat had been cast farther out into that mapless Mexican sea.

Who was lying? What really existed, what didn't? Who was anyone?—even Jorge, even herself. The need to survive crushed them all out of shape as easily as tin cans.

And, Christ Jesus, she hadn't even asked if Guadalupe's husband, Ramón, knew that she was dead. . . .

The rutted road around the reservoir's backside was almost a blessing. It forced her to concentrate, to focus her mind on something immediate as the pickup swayed and slammed its way back toward Obregón. The suitcase in the seat beside her bounced like a child. As long as she had that, she had one hope left—and she would use it.

In a stand of cottonwoods where the river began spreading out into the reservoir, she slid the pickup to a stop. She and Jorge had come here alone often when they were first married and later with the children. Jorge had told her that he had found the little cave high up on the riverbank when he was a child. He'd hidden whatever secret treasures he'd had then in it for weeks at a time, he said, and nobody had disturbed them. She didn't need weeks— only a day or a few hours, she thought as she slid down the riverbank with the heavy suitcase.

There was no sign of anyone's having been near the three-foot-high opening in a long time. She shoved the suitcase an arm's length back along the dry dirt, into the shadows. There was coolness there, and she thought how fine it would be to crawl in with the suitcase, to wait out the heat and red light. Then her eyes found the scorpion who apparently had been watching her the whole time, tail curled and poised, from the sun-heated rock above the cave's entrance. He was a reminder, an emblem. Keep going, keep going.

She backed away down the bank to the shallow river and washed some of the dried sweat and the dirt off her hands and face. The rest of her could wait.

As she started her climb up the path that led to the top of the bank, a spot of color caught her eye from across the river. She kept climbing, pretending not to notice, until the path cut back on itself and she could look across to the other high bank without seeming to stare. She was sure that the man who was watching her hadn't been there when she had hidden the suitcase—she'd made certain she was alone. He stood behind a low patch of cholla cactus, looking down at her and cradling his gun—a machine gun, she thought— loosely. He was just close enough for her to see from his face that his interest in her was mild, that she was only a diversion.

She glanced upriver at the sluice gates that she knew were the reason for the man's being there. Jorge had explained to her: use the river as we always have, but leave before sundown. They open the gates after dark and send the water flooding into the mari- juana fields. And they don't like to be watched. It didn't matter who "they" was, he'd told her. You didn't ask, you didn't want to know. All that mat- tered was that, in some kind of unspoken Mexican accommodation, the night belonged to whoever planted and protected those endless acres of marijuana that everyone knew and didn't know stretched away from this riverbank.

She didn't look at the man again after the path switched back. She checked the sun. It was already lowering into late afternoon.

Would the man be there after dark, watching as ready as the scorpion then, if she didn't make it back before the sun disappeared—if she made it back at all? But she knew she couldn't care about that now. There was no time to find another place for the suitcase. Nightfall was an eternity from now, something that would be waiting for her in another part of this deadly labyrinth Mexico had built for her. Patiently waiting.

Pebbles flew clattering up from the pickup's spinning wheels as she swung it into the ruts again, toward the city.

The old cars were gone from Alicia Dura's yard. The cats pretending to sleep, the silly puppies, the girl on the tricycle, the woman watching from across the street—all of them were gone. There was no faint band music from the center of town. The eucalyptus and palo verde trees threw long afternoon shadows now, and the reds and pinks of the oleander blossoms had been subtly changed, deepened, by the yellowing afternoon light. It was as if she'd come back to a place she'd once known years ago.

Aguilar's own need to protect himself protected her, too, she knew. That much of what he'd told her she believed: he couldn't afford to be seen here, to appear to be interfering. If he had anyone watching her, she didn't care. As long as watching was all he did.

The wooden door behind the screen was closed now. She stopped in front of it and strained for the sound of voices from inside. Nothing. For a moment she considered trying the handle, simply stepping inside. But she remembered Alicia's story of the men who had come for her father. She knew that if anybody was inside, they wouldn't take a chance on that happening again.

She knocked. Waited. Knocked again. Then she saw a small movement in the curtain at the window next to the door, and knew that someone had looked outside. After a moment, a lock on the door clicked.

When it swung open, the dimness of the entrance hall and the torn, dirty screen wouldn't let her make out who was inside. She recognized Carlos's quiet voice before his features came together for her. "I'm surprised," he said.

"I want to come in."

He flipped up the hook that held the screen closed and stepped back for her to let herself in. Then he turned and walked ahead of her into the living room. She saw an open book in a frayed easy chair. Only one lamp was lit, the one beside the chair. He'd been reading, damn him! Calmly reading, as if he weren't aware in the least that the world was exploding all around him.

But when he picked up the book to sit again, and

she saw the revolver under it, she knew he was perfectly aware. And she had a flash of admiration and envy that he could sit and read and wait.

"Where's my son?" she demanded.

"Where he should be. With Alicia."

"I have the money," she said. "I want him."

"The money's your affair. Where did you go today? I came back for you."

"Did you?"

"You were my responsibility. I came back."

"From where?"

"*Mira*, look. Before I left with Juan and Miranda in their truck, I came into the house for you. Three of your friends were there, so I couldn't go past the kitchen. Where were you?"

"They weren't my friends."

"Then how did you get out of there, if not with them. Nobody saw you outside the house."

"I was on the roof, damn it. I sat on the roof and passed out in the heat. If you don't believe that, I can't help it. I have the money and I want my son and I don't know or really care who raided your—my—lands today. And my housekeeper—my friend—is dead because your letter from that damned 'Game Committee' didn't work. You'll get your money when I get my son, or you'll never get it at all. Now *where is he*?"

He regarded her a long while. She was conscious of her breathing, quick with anger, in the silence of the room. "On the roof?" he said at length.

"And I came back down and finished digging the

money out. You can go check for yourself that it's gone.''

"I have no proof that it was ever there."

"It was *there*, damn you."

"As much as you thought?"

"More."

"And you were on the *roof*?"

"Yes, on the roof, yes!"

"And let me understand. You think that someone from Alicia's people wrote you that letter you showed us?''

"Tell me why it doesn't make sense. You 'negotiate' for our lands, then come up with a scheme to get our own money so you can buy our equipment from us. And then I walk in here and hand you my child to make sure nothing goes wrong! . . ." Yes, she thought. Please. Don't let it make sense.

He was silent again, thinking. "I can't tell you it doesn't."

"Then you did write it."

"I didn't say that. Personally, I know *I* didn't write it. About your housekeeper—I don't know anything. But I can't tell you it doesn't make sense for one of us to have written the letter. It does make perfectly good sense, if you think about it. So would you believe me if I told you none of us did?"

She considered. "No. No more than I can believe what the police told me."

"So?"

"I don't care what's true—please, I don't care now. Just tell me where my son is, that's all I want. *Please*."

104

"I can't."

"Why not?"

"Your *pistoleros* hit one of our camps last night, another this afternoon. One man's dead already—not one of theirs. We've got camps all over this valley. How long should Alicia sit here and talk and listen to my 'advising' before she goes out to her people? You want me to tell you just where she is so the next raid can go straight for her? It would be a hell of a lot easier to make her disappear out there than here, no?"

"Why aren't you with her?"

"They had to leave somebody behind in Obregón. I'm probably the least useful person they've got now. The local people don't know me well enough to trust me out there. And that was my suggestion, by the way."

"Then you don't really have to be here—you're not *doing* anything. You can take me to her. You'd be certain I didn't tell anybody where we're going."

He took off his glasses, touched the tips of the earpieces together, and absently studied them. He was thinking, and she felt a small spurt of hope.

"No," he said. "I can't. You don't belong there now."

"Dear God, my son's there, isn't he? Listen to me—you told me you didn't have the right to make any decisions. I'm telling you there's money involved now, more money than Alicia's ever had to work with in her life. It doesn't matter if she wrote the letter; I'm offering her the money. And the lands, the other

105

things I promised we wouldn't stand in her way about—I can convince her my promise is still good. You don't have any *right* to keep me away from her."

He paused again. "And once you know your boy's all right, what then?"

"Then I'll take you to the money, or you can keep me—anything. And as soon as I can reach my husband, your people can go back on our land. That's worth something, isn't it? No more fighting for it, nobody else dying. Just take me to my son. Just that. Please."

He put his glasses back on. Then he stood, picked up a newspaper from one of the dinette chairs, and folded it around the revolver. "When he left here with Alicia, your boy was fine," he said, his eyes not meeting hers. "For myself, I believe you were on the roof. But you're right. None of it's my decision." He switched off the lamp. The room was slashed by planes of late afternoon light from around the curtains, as if his action had set it free. "Your car's on the street behind us. But your pickup won't attract as much attention. We'll take that." He held out his hand for the keys.

Outside, the air smelled of supper already, of a hundred kinds of food being readied for the night's parties. Her throat tightened at the thought of food or celebration.

They drove westward toward the orange sun. Over the mountains to the west, a few late rainy-season thunderheads were too far away to promise anything but a brilliant sunset. Even in her pickup, they went slowly as a hay wagon, it seemed to her, as if Carlos were determined to attract no attention to himself. Habit, she decided, the habit of a man used to careful anonymity. He crept behind the slick-tired, faded trucks and the huge, crowded jalopies with Styrofoam dice dangling in their windows, trucks that carried *campesinos* home from the day's festivities to their adobe or cinder-block houses in the darkening countryside. When killer buses, or transport trucks with rainbow striping on their cabs and slogans like "Abandoned by God" on their bumpers roared up behind him, he practically drove off onto the crumbling shoulder to let them pass. In spite of her impatience and uncertainty, she relaxed a little into the motion of the ride. She had even slept once upon a time, she remembered, on clean sheets, in her own room. She tried to call the Vermont light back again, but the sun in front of her drove it away.

She had promised the money. And now what? If Comandante Aguilar had been lying, if the Sixteenth of September Committee had sent the letter after all, when would they be back? Had Guadalupe only been a warning that they would be? And if they did come back, and she'd given the money away, what would she do then? She could be throwing her last defense against them away, and all for one look at Luis.

Damn Jorge, damn him for not being here with her. Damn him for sitting in a hotel bar or a government office all day, trying to hold on to dirt. He should be here; suddenly she resented him so strongly that she felt a fury which left her hands gripping the seat until her knuckles whitened.

She saw that Carlos had noticed her hands, but he said nothing. She wanted him to. His presence there on the seat beside her, his placidity, his quiet were things she needed desperately. They were the kinds of things she had always gotten from Jorge. She wanted for a moment to touch Carlos, to see if she might somehow absorb them from him, like electric current. But she knew they were locked away from her, like almost everything else about the man.

She switched the radio on. An American rock song blared. He switched it off.

"Decadent?" she asked.

"No," he said. "Just annoying."

"None of that in Havana, I bet." If she couldn't have that placidity, she could at least crack it.

"Enough. Too much. Look, don't take it out on me. I'm helping you, remember? If you want to find Alicia on your own, fine."

She switched the radio on again, this time to the close harmonies and guitars of a *norteño* song. Somebody's woman had gone away, he was drunk, he was poor, his heart was trampled. She begrudged the singer his simple problems.

When they turned off the highway, she was puzzled. She didn't know this place. So far as she remembered, there was nothing but open fields anywhere around here. No one's country house existed for at least five miles in either direction.

Carlos must have seen her apprehension—or felt it. That was part of his quietness, too, she thought. That was why she'd been so uneasy when she was first in the room with him and Alicia. She was sure he *felt* things, kept quiet and still because he was listening to something most people couldn't hear. "Not everybody is as lucky as the people on your lands," he said, as if in answer to her puzzlement. "They had a house, something to start with. Sometimes you start with just the land."

At first she wasn't sure if what she saw ahead of them was only the swirls of dust devils the evening winds raised. But as they wallowed farther along the road—the trail through the fields—she was sure they weren't. She made out individual columns, the smoke rolling up cleanly for a time, then being caught by the still-hot breeze and whipped away.

"Go faster," she said.

But already the pickup had lurched as Carlos dropped it down a gear, and it surged forward through the mine field potholes of the road.

An adobe hut, a well, two sheds woven from ocotillo limbs, a single mesquite tree. A stake where a dog or a burro had been tied. A score of straw windbreaks, mostly heaps of ashes by now. Homemade tables, broken. Enameled or tin pots and pans, dented or bullet riddled. Pieces of clothing, crawling slowly away in the wind. Fluttering school notebooks. Rubble of smashed plates and cups. The smell of smoke, the rushing sound of the wind through cornfields. The distant thunderheads. And above her, a red sunset that stretched from horizon to horizon, coloring the whole sky.

She knelt and picked up a child's picture book, one of the cheap superhero books Jorge would never let Luis buy in the newsstands. "Luis," she said loudly into the emptiness. Then again, shouting it as if he could have heard her, "Luis!"

The wind gusted, clattered a loose piece of tin on the adobe hut. Smoke stung her eyes.

Carlos stepped up behind her. He rested his hand lightly on her shoulder and she let it stay.

"I'm hungry," she said, so low she wondered if he could hear her over the wind. "I'm so very hungry."

Three

ALICIA WON'T BE BACK HERE," HE SAID TO
her, "but somebody will."

"How do you know?" she asked.

"When you don't have much, you salvage what
you can."

"And what if somebody does come back?"

"Then we at least know what happened. Maybe

where Alicia went. Maybe whose men were here. That's a place to start."

"I want to go back to her house."

"She won't be there."

"How can you be sure?"

"She can't do any good from there. If she managed to get away, she's on her way to other camps. They have to be warned."

"With my son?"

"I don't know."

"And what if she didn't get away?"

"I don't know."

"They could tell Luis didn't belong here. They wouldn't have hurt him."

"Probably not."

"Do you think that? Do you really think that?"

"I don't know."

"I want to look for him."

"There's no place to look. We have to stay here. We have to wait."

She let him convince her. No, she knew he was right, and that convinced her. If strength was what she had to find in herself again, she knew it had to be the strength to wait—the greatest strength of all.

In the wreck of the camp they'd found a half-empty bag of rice, a dented can of refried beans, and a tin pot whose lower half, at least, was intact. From behind the seat of the truck, she had taken Jorge's "emergency stash" that he kept in case he got stuck in the fields late: two cans of Vienna sausages, a box of crackers, and a pint of home-brew *bacanora* tequila.

Her hunger was real. She needed the strength eating would bring, yes. But beyond that, the isolation of this place, the sense that everything else in the world but the wind in the cornstalks had stopped for a while, had somehow made eating the only thing that mattered now. In the city where she could be moving, be *doing* something, food had been unthinkable.

While he built a new fire in front of the doorway to the adobe hut from the remains of the old one, she went behind the hut and washed in tepid well water—not the scrubbing she'd promised herself, but not just hands and face, either. She drew up bucket after bucket and let it stream over her gritty hair, down into all the crevices of her body in the last of the daylight. The wind dried her, a warm, dry wind just at the edge of turning cool for the night. She stood still a long time and let it curl around her, like hands.

She heated the beans and boiled the rice almost without speaking. As the wind turned cooler, the fire began to feel good, and the swigs of *bacanora* they each took drove away some of the coldness inside that had stayed with her even through the hottest part of the day. As they ate, Kathleen not tasting the food, leaning against the walls of the hut as a windbreak, she felt the food and the *bacanora* slipping into her muscles like a drug. She felt almost as if she were in a tub of hot water, weightless, floating. Her mind slowed, and for whole seconds at a time she was able to let herself imagine that nothing at all existed outside the circle of firelight, that she was watching a campfire beside the green pond at the summerhouse on a July

114

night. And that she had no children, that Obregón didn't exist, that the man who sat on the other side of the doorway from her was someone she'd known a long time, might even have thought about being in love with.

But these seconds of forgetfulness weren't enough. In spite of her terrible fatigue, she was almost wild with waiting. Each time the fire leapt up, it was a signal that another minute, another minute in which she'd done nothing, had passed. The waiting was like a physical pressure, something pressing on her chest and threatening to collapse it. She had to fill those minutes and seconds somehow, fill the empty spaces in herself. Talk would do it, she knew, talk about what she didn't care, just as long as there were words to batter against the emptiness.

She mixed a little of the *bacanora* with well water and drank it. "You don't have a family," she said to Carlos.

"No." He'd taken his glasses off and was staring into the fire.

"Did you ever?"

"In San Francisco."

"American?"

"Yes. From a town called Chico, north of there."

"Children?"

"A girl."

"How old?"

"Ten now."

"You don't like to talk about it?"

He shrugged lightly. "I was in school. My father

was a lawyer, in politics. Crooked as most, I suppose. He sent me to Berkeley. We met, we got married, we had a baby. Then the time came for me to come back to Mexico. She didn't want to.''

''You mean they were going to deport you?''

''No. I could have stayed. It was just time.''

The *bacanora* settled. She never wanted to leave this circle of light, never wanted to move again, as long as the words kept coming to make her forget the waiting. ''What does that mean?''

''I thought I would stay when I met her. I wanted to make documentary films, do social work, something fuzzy like that—things people in your country do to convince themselves they're honest. I could have stayed. But I would never have *been* American, even though I was living like one. I don't suppose that makes much sense.''

''Yes. Yes, it does.''

He looked at her for the first time. ''And you've never wanted to go home?''

''I do go sometimes.''

''That's not what I meant.''

''I know it wasn't. All right, yes, I've wanted to go home a thousand times. When I first married Jorge, I thought about it less than I have since the children came. My own father is a teacher—honest as most, I suppose—in a little college in a town from a postcard, and I never lived anywhere else. There are gravestones with my mother's family name on them in the next town over that go back two hundred years. It's

116

not easy to cut yourself off from that—or to cut your children off from it."

"That letter said your children were in school there."

"It's not the same."

"No. There's Mexican blood in them now."

She flinched, and hoped he didn't see it. "You can be very small, can't you."

He shrugged. "All I know is what my own wife's family thought."

"That's why you really left the States, isn't it?" She waited for him to drop his eyes from hers, but he didn't. It was as if he were telling her that nothing she could say could really get through to him, not to any place that mattered. It seemed to her that he let her step close for a moment just to give himself the opportunity to shove her away. She couldn't tell if he was reacting to *her* or to some private thing she stood for. And she knew that meant she had absolutely no way of predicting how he *would* react, and that both frightened her and fascinated her.

"Look," he said. "When you're young, you try on lives, like different styles of clothing. If you're lucky, you find one that fits you before you get married, have children, decide where you think you want to settle, what you're going to do with your future. If you're not, you take off the old life. That's all."

"That's all?"

"No. It can hurt like hell when you do. Don't try it just for some gravestones with a family name on them."

He turned to the fire again. "I'm sorry," she said.

"Don't be. I made a choice, you made a different choice. You've stayed here. Why?"

She took another sip of the *bacanora* and leaned her head back against the rough adobe wall. It pulled at her hair, and little bits of adobe flaked away and sifted down her shirt collar. Why had she stayed? She could tell him all about conscious compromises and her children and sticking by your choices, she supposed. Or she could let it go with some very reasonable remark about knowing she might never be able to see her children again if she left and Jorge didn't. Or try to explain the equally true reason that if she went back to Vermont she would feel as if she were crawling beneath one of those gravestones, the way she had always imagined generations of women like her mother had done as soon as they grew up into that fixed, gray world of theirs.

But what about the reason that was stronger than any of those? How did she go about telling him the way Jorge's hands had felt when they first made love in Arizona those dozen years ago. And that, even here, she could feel them on her if she closed her eyes. How in God's name did she tell him that she loved the stupid way Jorge sometimes managed to have long conversations with dogs, or the way he somehow could keep the friendship of men like Enrique and the respect of people like Alicia Dura? That she trusted him, even when she knew he was wrong she trusted him. That he always managed to *be there* for her . . .

Until now. Goddamn it, *where was Jorge,* she

thought, and she felt the unreasoning, angry tension that had tightened her hands in the truck coming back. And the pressure of the waiting swelling again. She glanced over at Carlos and tried to imagine the feel of Jorge's body against hers, the quietness and warmth of it. For a moment, she wondered what would happen if she put the *bacanora* down and reached over and touched Carlos, as she'd wanted to do in the truck. Would he feel like Jorge? Could she make him feel like Jorge if she just took another drink of *bacanora* and closed her eyes and let the warmth take over?

Then Carlos drew his legs up and flung a handful of twigs onto the fire, and the moment disappeared into the shower of sparks the twigs made. But not the memory of Jorge's hands, of his face in the faces of their children.

"Why did I stay?" she said. "Long story. Maybe I'm old-fashioned. Or maybe those clothes still fit— enough of them do, at least."

He nodded. In the silence, the wind rose. There was a clear chill in it now, enough to break through the warmth of the fire and seem to shrink the circle of firelight. She took a sip of *bacanora* straight from the bottle and passed it to him.

"Did you expect me to be surprised when you told me you'd lived in Havana?" she said, to keep voices filling up the darkness.

"You mean because of some nonsense like wanting to shock your bourgeois sensibilities? Or whatever undergraduates call them nowadays. No, not particularly.''

Your point, she thought. "Why *did* you go there, if it was time to come back to Mexico?"

"When I came home, I saw that I didn't have the slightest idea what Mexico was all about. Then when I found out, when I saw how much there was to do, I went somewhere that promised to teach me how to do it. It's not complicated.''

"Did they?''

He shrugged again. "I told you before. Some of it. But so did San Francisco. I'm still trying to work it out.'' He passed the *bacanora* back to her and she took it, but put it down on the ground beside her.

"Will we stay here all night?'' she said.

"I don't think we'll have to. Somebody will come.''

They were silent again. He put more wood on the fire, broken pieces of furniture, split hoe handles. Even the *bacanora* wasn't holding in the warmth. "I want to go inside,'' she said. "Out of the wind.''

He glanced at the dark interior of the hut. "You have a flashlight in the truck?''

"I think so.''

After a moment, he got up and from the darkness she heard the truck door open. Somewhere coyotes sang to each other, celebrating a kill. Could there be a sound that would make this place seem more desolate than that one?

The beam of the flashlight swept the bare ground in front of him like the single eye of a locomotive as he came back. He aimed it into the hut for her. For some reason—probably because it belonged to the land-owner—the hut had been left alone. A pallet and a half dozen cardboard boxes full of clothes and blankets took up much of the space. She pulled a blanket from a box and spread it on the pallet. He stayed in the door with the light. The sense of floating, the warmth, kept slipping away.

"Do you want to sleep?" he asked her.

"Yes," she said. "No. That would be the worst thing."

"Then rest." He stepped into the room and knelt to smooth the blanket for her, then turned it back. It was a gesture so unexpected, so out of the character she'd given him, that in another time and place she might have cried. He stood, and as he did he brushed her arm.

"Sorry," he said.

The touch, even that slight touch, had brought some of the warmth back. He reached out and touched her temple lightly and again she wondered, what would it be like, could she make this nameless man into Jorge? Could she hide in him for one long night? He took a step closer to her.

She stepped back away from him. No. Jorge had a name, a face, a self. She wanted *Jorge*. She had to hold on to something outside this nightmare, didn't she? Carlos belonged to this place, the sound of those coyotes, the cold wind of this night. Did she want that to become part of her?

She looked at him in the spill of light from the flash. His face was a stranger's, in a hundred ways.

She took his hand and pressed it. "Thanks," she said. "Keep the light. I won't need it."

He held her hand for a few seconds, then dropped it when she let it go limp in his. "I'll be outside," he said.

She lay on the pallet and watched the ocotillo ribs of the hut's roof move in the small light from the fire outside. When she was sure Carlos was settled, she moved her hand down her stomach, and beyond, and let it rest there. Damn you, Jorge, she thought. I love you. Help me find our son! The warmth slowly faded, and she listened to the distant sound of the coyotes, listened and waited for other noises that would tell her people had come back and it was time to begin again to play the other, more deadly game she knew she had to finish.

When she checked the glowing numbers of her watch, it was eight o'clock. She had been here nearly two hours, and nothing had changed but the deepening night. The tense rest had drained some of the weariness out of her, like a poison, but she felt heavy and slow when she went back outside to the fire, as if she were walking under water.

"Do you think the fire's frightening them away?" she asked Carlos, who was sitting closer to the fire now.

"No. They know the *pistoleros* are gone."

Then now what, she thought. More waiting, more staring at the ceiling, more fatigue that grew until the

waiting would be almost a relief, more hopelessness?
More fear?

"I don't care about what good it does," she said.
"I've got to start looking for him. Anywhere, even if
I just drive up and down the highway."

He got to his feet, silhouetted against the firelight.
"Do you want to find your boy or do you want to
make yourself feel better?"

She turned away from him, angry because she knew
what he said was true. "All right," she said. "At
least I can look around here." She bent and picked
up the flashlight from the ground beside him.

"For what?"

"For anything, I don't know. Just to move." She
walked past him, half expecting him to follow her.
When he didn't, she was disappointed but kept going.
She was making herself feel better, not him. Why
should he be foolish, too?

She moved the flashlight in a long arc to get her
bearings. The mesquite tree was to her right, the road
and truck straight ahead. The smoldering heaps that
had been windbreaks were everywhere. She moved
the flashlight in a slower arc the second time, keeping
its beam focused on the rows of ripe corn that surrounded the clearing like a low forest. She looked for
a broken stalk, leaves torn, anything that would tell
her which direction the people had gone. To her left
one whole swatch of stalks was ripped out, leaving a
stubbly opening wide as a house. The pickups and
four-by-fours would have come in from there, as they

had at the country house. Whoever had been here before surely wouldn't have run that way.

She walked to her right. As she got closer to the corn rows she saw that, yes, here and there stalks were broken, ears of corn lay between the rows. At one place she found what might have been blood on one of the sharp leaves. But there was no pattern to anything, no sign that most of the people had gone any particular way. When they had fled, it had been in disorganized panic.

She looked behind her. Carlos stood patiently by the fire, head lowered, absorbed in the flames. She turned back to the fields. A half-moon was rising, spreading a watery glow over the corn tassles whipping in the wind. He could be out there, she thought suddenly. Luis could be out there. He could be hurt.

She chose the nearest break in the corn, at random, and plunged into it. She felt the sting of the leaves as they whipped at her, felt clods of dirt crumbling beneath her sandals. She swung the light ahead of her rapidly as she went, so rapidly that it seemed to be a single bright arc. She found more broken stalks, more loose ears, and tried to make them define a path for her. But there was no path, only erratic, crisscrossing breaks in the forest of stalks, places where people had circled and turned, running away like foxes from dogs.

She didn't know how far she had gone before she realized that she, too, hadn't been traveling in a straight line. She looked at her watch and saw that it was eight-fifteen. How much distance could she have traveled in fifteen minutes? She moved the light around her in a complete circle. In every direction, the beam found nothing but green stalks and leaves and brown cornsilk rippling like seaweed in the wind. Even if there had been trees to use as landmarks, like the Italian cypresses at the country house, they would have been useless to her. The plants seemed twice her height. Not even the low moon was visible above their tops, not the glow from Carlos's fire.

These fields were almost unbroken by hills or streams, were deliberately kept free of walls or hedgerows or trees so that the giant farm machines could roam them unhindered. They might go for miles.

She caught her breath and started back in the direction she thought she'd come. But she'd gone only a score of paces before she realized she had turned somewhere around here, following what she had believed was a trail of footprints. But the footprints had stopped as abruptly as they had begun. And which way had she turned?

"Carlos!" she shouted into the wind, and waited.

"Carlos!" Louder this time. She strained to hear an answer. The wind eased. Still nothing. It picked up again.

She was certain, though, she'd heard another sound just as it picked up, the sound of something moving far more jerkily than the wind. And something lower down in the corn. She tried to place where it had come from, but couldn't. "Carlos?" she said, her voice straining to keep an even pitch. Then, "Luis?"

Could he really be there? The sound came from

somewhere near the ground. Could he have seen her light, not be able to walk—be crawling toward her? A billion to one chance, yes, but it could be. It *could*.

She swung the light wildly around her. And there, to her left—something dark, and she was sure it had moved. She crashed across rows toward it, her arm folded in front of her face to protect herself from the sharp leaves. The dark thing moved again. She ran, stumbled through more rows. And then she was aware that the dark thing was moving away from her, not toward her, moving far faster than a hurt child could. She stopped, panting, and knelt to steady the light. It caught just for the briefest moment the thin, gray form of a coyote dodging away through the rows, the feet of a jackrabbit dangling from its mouth.

Even in the wind, sweat stung the tiny cuts the corn leaves had left on her hands and face. She got to her feet, feeling foolish but disappointed, too. Where now? Would she panic like the people whose trails she'd believed she was following, and chase more coyotes? Or start out along a corn row that could take her until midnight to find the end of, and then maybe come out even farther into this ridiculous maze she'd gotten herself trapped in?

"Carlos!" she tried again.

"Buenas noches, señora." The voice came from her right—or she thought there had been a voice. It sounded like a man's voice, but one so high she couldn't be certain.

"Quién habla?" she said, her own voice pitched tight as a telegraph wire. "Who's talking?" Aim the

light, she told herself. *See* who's talking. But her arm was stone.

"*Aquí.* Over here."

"Come into the light."

"*Cómo no.* Of course."

The sound of the sea of corn parting jerked her out of her paralysis. She swept the light toward the sound.

"*Gracias, señora.* That's better now."

Now she could tell there were two figures, one leading the other by the hand through the corn. For a moment she didn't recognize the figure behind because the woman's curlers were gone. But when she made out the Caterpillar baseball cap on the man and then the woman's I ♥ Los Angeles T-shirt, torn now, she said a quick prayer to all the corn gods of Mexico.

"Señora Zaragoza, no?" the Caterpillar cap said.

"Yes. . . ."

"Juan and Miranda Diaz, to serve you, señora. Remember?"

"And Alicia? Is Alicia with you?"

"No, señora. Unhappily, no." They stopped a few feet from her, and she was aware that she was shining the light in Juan's face, like an interrogator. She quickly lowered it.

"Where is she?"

They both began to speak at once. Juan stopped and left it to Miranda, whose words spewed out like buckshot. "She was with us when we ran in here, señora. And then she wasn't. We've been in here ever since, all of us. *Pues* some of us may have gone home, but most of us are here. Juan and I are going ahead to see if it's all right. Is it all right, señora?" Even though the flashlight beam was no longer in their faces, Miranda's eyes were squinting, trying to see Kathleen behind the light. There was suspicion in them.

Fine. Miranda had a right to be suspicious. But Carlos could explain later, could explain everything he wanted to, or nothing at all. "Nobody but Carlos is there. My son—was my son with Alicia?"

"He was, señora. But afterward, after we lost Alicia . . . we couldn't know." She paused the length of a breath, and the suspicion eased in her eyes as she found a common ground with Kathleen. "What a precious little boy!"

"Could the *pistoleros* have gotten to Alicia—or to my son? Do you know?"

"We left our truck and Alicia's car by the highway, señora. They're gone now. Maybe Alicia took one of them. Maybe the *pistoleros* did. *Quién sabe?* Who knows?"

Kathleen's anger surged. "Yes, somebody knows. Not *quién sabe*—*some*body in that bunch of yours has to have seen something. . . ."

"I'm sorry," Juan broke in. "We've talked about it, all of us. Nobody saw. We were all running. Some of us were hurt, and we had to help them, señora."

"All right, the *pistoleros*. Who were they?" She was ashamed of her anger, but helpless to stop it.

"*Quién sa*—" Juan began.

Miranda cut him off. "The same ones as before, señora."

"But no one knows for sure who they are," Juan said.

"Marta Vasquez said she thought she knew one of them," Miranda went on. "Marta was a waitress, and she said he used to come into the restaurant."

"She said she wasn't sure, Miranda."

"No. Her husband said she wasn't sure. Marta didn't."

"Then who were they?" Kathleen's voice rose as if she and the woman were speaking different, utterly incomprehensible languages.

"Enrique Crouse's men, Marta says, señora." Miranda said, suddenly grave. "I believe her."

They came in a cautious procession out of the corn forest behind herself and Juan and Miranda. Most were silent, except the babies. Even the children seemed to sense the somberness, and only whispered among themselves as they spread out with their mothers and fathers to heaps of ashes and began poking in them for anything salvageable. Some of the *campesinos* carried a moaning woman with a ragged bandage covering one eye into the adobe hut, and then an unconscious man who breathed shallowly and heavily through his mouth. Kathleen gave them her flashlight, then stood back out of the way in the darkness beside the hut. Carlos brought the truck up and turned on its headlamps, which lit up the whole clearing like stark floodlights.

Enrique Crouse's men. Hope and confusion. Could

one of Enrique's "ears" have found out that Luis was here—that she was coming, too? And could Enrique have had a change of heart? Could he have sent his men for her here tonight, have sent them for her today at the country house? Why else—what possible reason—could he have had for sending them to these two particular places? It couldn't be coincidence. He always got his own back, but the country house wasn't even his!

That had to be it. Somehow—through Comandante Aguilar probably—Enrique had found out that the Game Committee wasn't involved after all. Aguilar had been telling the truth! And now even through her numbing fatigue, even in spite of the terrible, stupid hopelessness she'd felt when she was lost in that maze of corn, like the forest of lies she'd struggled with all day, she felt a small hope surge. Enrique had sent his men for her. And even though he had missed her, he might have Luis!

A girl slightly younger than Luis, hand clutching the remains of a stick of sugarcane, ran past her toward the dark beyond the hut. Kathleen stooped and put out an arm to stop her. The girl looked at her in surprise a moment, then let herself be turned back toward the light. Kathleen watched her go with a stab of urgency.

Don't be a fool, she told herself. Enrique might have Luis now, but so might Alicia. So might anyone else—Miranda had only said she *thought* the gunmen had been Enrique's. The Game Committee could still be involved, Aguilar might have been lying, Carlos might have been, Alicia might have been . . . she could be as lost as ever. And Luis even more lost than ever.

In the cold moonlight, she looked at the hand she'd used to stop the girl and saw it was shaking. She tried to get up from her stooped position and couldn't. The shaking spread from her hands through her whole body now, and she doubled over and hugged her knees. She squeezed her eyes shut against the images that tried to crowd up in front of them.

She drove them away by picturing Alicia Dura's face. There was nothing in that face to say that she would do anything vicious or vindictive. As long as Kathleen kept her part of the bargain about the lands, as long as she could still offer Alicia the money for her people, Luis would be safe with her. If she still had him.

Alicia was somewhere. Only somewhere, in another desolate squatters' camp like this one, warning, organizing. Kathleen knew where Enrique was. Even if he didn't have Luis, even if he'd only changed his mind and decided to help her, he was the one she had to find first. And if it became necessary, surely one of his "ears" could find out where Alicia was.

She opened her eyes and used the rough adobe wall of the hut to steady herself as she got to her feet. By the fire she and Carlos had built, Carlos and Juan and Miranda were deep in some sort of mumbled conference. When she came into the light and approached them they broke off and looked up at her, vaguely hostile in the stark light, almost as if she had been a schoolteacher who'd caught them doing something shameful.

"I want to go back," she said, focusing on Carlos.

No one answered her. The comforting calm she'd found in Carlos's face was no longer comforting in the harsh light from the headlamps. It was the cold calm of stone.

"I have to go back. I have to find him."

"Who, señora?" Carlos's señora cut her with its sarcasm.

"Luis," she said. "Of course, Luis."

"Ah," Carlos said. "Luis. Not you husband."

"My husband is in Mexico City. You know that."

Miranda's voice was soft, almost apologetic. "No, señora."

"I spoke to him this morning. I know he's in Mexico City."

"Maybe this morning, señora. Not this afternoon."

"What do you mean?" She turned on Miranda, wondering that she still had the strength for surprise.

"We went back to your country house before we came out here—after you had left. We saw him, señora."

"You *saw* him? You saw Jorge?"

"*Sí.*"

"That's a lie."

Carlos broke in. "There's no reason for them to lie."

Kathleen ignored him. "Why didn't you tell me in the fields?"

"We wanted to talk to Carlos," Juan said. "We

wanted to find out if he knew about your husband, too."

"Did you?" Kathleen said to Carlos.

"No. But I think you did."

Kathleen took a step back from them, then whirled and faced the lights from the pickup, breathing the glare in, letting it blind her. "Yes, you'd think that. Then tell me—*you* tell me why I knew my husband is in Obregón. If he is."

Carlos's voice came evenly above the hushed conversation of the other *campesinos* in the clearing. "You knew the government would give us the land anyway, eventually. But our people got to it sooner than you'd thought. Your husband had planned to 'negotiate' with Alicia, hadn't he?—and you thought there was no hurry. But he charged off to Mexico City and didn't get her note in time, so we were on the land before he had a chance to get his money out of your country house. He came back for it—after he'd had his friend Enrique drive us off. But you'd gotten there before him." He spoke as if he were reciting something from memory, something that he had actually seen himself. Yes, she thought, he probably did see the world that way, a world of plots and counterplots. Was that what it took to survive as a good revolutionary? All that calm, that quiet—it was only his waiting for the falseness, the treachery he was sure would come sooner or later. And that made him dangerous in a way she hadn't understood.

His voice went on as assured as before. "Was it a mix-up? Did he get here too late? Or was the whole

Game Committee letter your own idea? Like the story about being on the roof, for God's sake—which I believed. And then you were supposed to get me out here in time for your friend Enrique's raid, so that those bastards of his could get everything wrapped up all at once—take your boy back for you, then get Alicia and myself both in one neat raid out here where nobody could ever prove anything. What good thinking, señora, what a fine plan! But we're Mexicans, aren't we? We have this problem with time—we're always a little too late or a little too early. And twice today, our problem with time ruined what you had set up so wonderfully and with such *gringo* precision. My apologies, señora. All that trouble ruined—all that talk about families and home you did to make me feel at ease with you. What a pity."

He sounded so satisfied, she thought, that the world had turned out as he'd expected it would again. "You saw my son," she said. "Do you think I would use him that way? Would I put him in that kind of danger?"

"I don't know what people like you might do. I've never been people like you."

"People like what? People who love their children?" She turned back to the fire. After the glare of the headlamps, the three around it were only shapes, as the coyote had been. "Miranda. Tell him. Would you do that to one of your children?"

"I'm not a *gringa*, señora. I've never known a *gringa* besides you."

"Does that make me a monster? Would you do that to one of your children, just tell me that!"

134

"No."

"And you, Juan. Would you let her do it?"

Juan poked at the fire, and it sent up a puff of ashes and smoke. "I don't understand why your husband is here, señora. I wish I knew another reason."

"I don't understand either—I swear to you I don't. But if I can get back to Obregón, I can find out. Help me get back—please help me get back."

Carlos stood. "Come here. I'm going to show you something." He disappeared into the hut for a moment and came out with the flashlight. He rounded the hut toward the rear, then waited for her to follow. She hesitated. "Will you get me back to town?" she said.

"Don't try to bargain with me," he said. "I don't know what I'll do—but whatever it is, I'm going to show you this first."

She threw a quick glance at Juan and Miranda. Neither of them looked up from the fire. "Miranda," she said, low enough so that Carlos couldn't hear—she hoped. "Miranda, I want my child."

Miranda's eyes darted up to hers for a part of a second, too small a part for Kathleen to read anything there. But her hope flickered, stayed alive. "I'm coming," she said to Carlos.

As she followed him along a sandy dry wash that led away from the hut toward the mountains, she knew that she ought to be afraid of him. He had power over her, and power here was to be feared. He was the only man who could have taken her to Alicia and Luis this afternoon. He was still the only human being who could see that she got to Luis and perhaps even to Jorge. But now if he believed that she had tricked him, used him, too, what could he justify doing?

Was there a point when you were so tired that even fear was blunted, the way pain was when you were too tired to care about it anymore? Or was it a kind of shock she'd slipped into? Jorge might be in Obregón. What did that mean? She should have felt relief, greater surprise. But it was as if that was one new piece of information too many, one new thing she simply couldn't try to make sense out of right now. She had to keep following this nameless man in front of her, had to do what he told her to, had to do whatever it took to get back out of these fields and to that street of white houses where Enrique was, where Luis might be, where even Jorge might be, where help could be.

Carlos stopped and turned so sharply that she thought for a moment he was going to hit her.

"Do you recognize it?" he said. The light was aimed at a wall of shoulder-high bushes, hidden from the clearing by the sea of cornstalks. So far as she could tell, the bushes stretched from here all the way to the base of the mountains.

She stepped closer, until she could see the clusters of thin, saw-toothed leaves. "Yes. It's marijuana." She spoke as matter-of-factly as she could. Did he want her to be shocked? No, she wouldn't give him that.

"It's not the land your friend Enrique cares about,

not all that corn, is it? The land will still be here tomorrow, and so will the corn. But he's afraid this won't be. *He's* afraid it won't, and your husband and the whole bunch of them are, too. People are starving here, kids' bellies are bloating, and the land is being used for *this*. And you want me to believe there's no connection between this and you and your husband and the things that have happened today? You really want me to say yes, I'll take you back into town and give up the only hand we might have to play now?"

"This is on my husband's land, too?"

"Why not?"

"Do you *know* it is? Have you seen it?"

"No. I don't have to."

"Yes, damn you, you do have to. Is that what Havana taught you? Nobody's different?"

He shrugged. "In some ways they aren't. It doesn't matter. It's all of a piece."

"What is that supposed to mean?"

"That only a fool would take you back to your husband now. You may be our only protection. Here you're useful. There you wouldn't be."

"Useful!"

He abruptly swung the light away from the marijuana plants and brushed past her toward the clearing. "Somebody will get into town eventually. They'll find out about your husband for you. And about your son." He stopped. "I'll see that this is burned. I hate to burn good cash crops, but if it's the only way to get your friends to leave us alone, I will. Once that's done, we won't need you anymore. My apologies if it cuts into your income." He started walking again.

She watched the light recede along the wash. "You're a pig," she said to his back.

He stopped again. "Have you considered," he said slowly, "what it means if your husband is back and you truly didn't know anything about it? Why would he have come home without telling you?"

"If Jorge's in Obregón, there's a good reason." She said it automatically, the way she'd said Hail Marys once to keep the wrong thoughts away.

"If there's not, you may be better off here with us," he said. "You're alive, at least. Think about that."

No, there was no reason for Juan and Miranda to have lied. They would know Jorge by sight, the way all the people who had worked for him did. If they were certain they saw him, then they had seen him—period.

Jorge was in town, then. And this morning he either hadn't known he was coming, or he had lied to her. Period, too. Why shouldn't that seem stranger to her than it did? She was certain she knew Jorge as well as any human being did. Less than an hour ago she'd wanted nothing so much as for him to be with her. And now he had done something totally beyond her ability even to begin to explain—and it didn't seem strange to her, the way it would have just yesterday. Did some of that money she'd risked so much for today come from drugs? She might even have something to fear from her own husband if Carlos was right, and even that didn't seem strange.

It was because of the way her tiredness distorted everything, yes, made the world come to her through thick, almost opaque glass. But she knew there was more. If she no longer was sure about which Kathleen *she* was, how could she pretend to be sure about Jorge—about anything?

Except Luis. And later a phone call to Vermont, when somehow she would be able to tell her father that *none* of her children was in danger any longer. She would make that call. She *would*. That mattered. That made the only sense. She had to hold on to it, like sanity.

Juan was wandering among the other *campesinos* when they reached the clearing again, giving advice, helping with windbreaks. But Miranda still sat by the fire, her eyes lost in it. Kathleen stopped beside her, and when Carlos had gone ahead into the hut and Juan had followed him, she squatted down next to her. Miranda didn't look up, but Kathleen knew she was aware of her. "Miranda?" she said after a time.

"I don't think you would do it, señora," Miranda said, her voice barely above a whisper. "I don't think you would use that little boy that way. *Por Dios*, he can't even talk!"

"I want him back, Miranda. That's all."

"I don't understand anything. I don't know what all this about letters and money is, and about your

139

husband and Enrique Crouse. I've just heard parts of things, and I don't know what's happening."

"Would you like me to explain?"

"No, señora. I think Alicia should know all that's happening. I want Alicia to explain. Not Carlos, not you—Alicia."

"You don't know where she is. That's the truth?"

"It's the truth, señora."

"What if I might be able to stop the raids? What if I might be able to find out where Alicia is, Miranda?"

"It would be the only thing, señora. That would be the only thing that can help now."

"Then you help *me* do it."

Miranda looked at her. "You want to find your husband?" The suspicion had come back into her voice.

"Yes. At least I hope I do."

"Where would you look for him?"

"Not at home. He wouldn't just wait there if he doesn't know what's happened to Luis and myself. I think I know that about him."

"No, Juan wouldn't be at home either. I believe that."

"But if he's in Obregón, I know who could tell me where he is."

"Who, señora?"

"Enrique Crouse."

Miranda turned back to the fire and spat into it. The fire made a sharp, quick hiss. "Not that one. I won't help anybody but the devil get to that one."

"Listen to me, Miranda. I made a promise to Alicia.

If something happens to me, there'll be nobody to see that it's kept. And it's a promise that you—all of you—will be better off for."

"What promise, señora?"

Kathleen explained. As she did, Miranda watched her for anything behind the words as much as she listened to the words themselves. Her own face kept vague suspicion in it, and an illegible reserve. When Kathleen was done, she said, "And you really don't care about all that land?"

"Not as much as I do about my family. This morning I was going to fight to keep it all. This morning was a long time ago."

Miranda considered, then nodded. "Do you want to leave Mexico?"

"I'll miss things. But yes, I know I have to."

"People who aren't in their countries are sad, no? The ones I know who have gone over there—" she motioned north, toward the border, "always say they carry their country around with them. You belong in your own country, señora." She seemed embarrassed by what she'd said, and made much of gathering a handful of useless twigs and tossing them into the fire. "*Mira,* señora. We had our truck and Alicia's car here. We parked them by the highway, out of sight behind some mesquite trees so nobody would know we were here. If Alicia got away from Enrique Crouse's men, she did it in her car. I don't know whether our truck is still there."

"You didn't go look?"

"No. What if the *pistoleros* had found them and

were waiting for us there?'' She pitched another handful of twigs. "But by now the *pistoleros* would be gone, no?''

The flicker of hope Kathleen had felt when she had seen Miranda glance at her before kindled and flared. Miranda went on. "If Enrique Crouse's men are coming back, then they'll come whether you're in Obregón or not. But maybe your husband can stop him. Alicia never said the kinds of things about your husband that she did about the other landowners. *Quién sabe*, señora? *Quién sabe?* I think Carlos likes to run things too much sometimes, and that's Alicia's job.''

"Will you take me, Miranda? Will you?"

Miranda shook her head. "I have to stay here with Juan and our people. And then we'll go back onto your land. You know that, don't you, señora?''

"Yes.''

"Carlos says we're going to burn the marijuana fields. Somebody will go for gasoline, then we'll burn the fields.'' She gave Kathleen the hint of a smile, a conspirator's smile. "But first he and Juan will talk about it for half an hour. Under the front bumper of our truck, there's a little box with a magnet. There's a key in the box. Do you understand?''

"I understand.''

"Follow the wash," Miranda said. "Straight along there.'' She pointed off to the right, where the wash sliced through the corn away from the marijuana fields toward the highway. "Just before the road you'll see the truck—if it's still there.''

Kathleen reached for her hand to thank her. Mi-

142

randa let her take it, but looked uncomfortable, as if that created a greater bond between them than she was sure she wanted. Kathleen let it go.

"I want you to have your boy back, señora," Miranda said. "And I want to have a little land in peace for my own children. Keep your promise."

"Your truck," Kathleen said as she got to her feet. "Where will I leave it?"

"At Alicia's, at your house—we'll find it."

The tight jeans and the squatting had left Kathleen's legs tingling. She squinted against the headlights at the wall of cornstalks and thought of the dark wash, the coyote she'd seen, the possibility that Carlos would find her gone too soon and come after her. Could she even run now if she had to? My God, to run, to drive back into Obregón, to force herself to keep thinking, acting—the very notion of it overwhelmed her. She glanced at her watch and saw that already it was nearly nine-thirty. At home, in another life, she would be winding down for bed.

She started directly for the boundary line of the cornfield. None of the other *campesinos* gave her more than a curious glance. But just before she reached the wash, she turned back in a long arc toward the rough road that led from the clearing to the highway. She would be behind her pickup there, behind the glare of the headlamps and hidden, she hoped.

Carlos had left the engine running. Any noise she made ought to be covered. Nonetheless, she eased the door open carefully. How easy it would be just to get in and drive away, she thought. But she was far too close to the others to try that from here.

The newspaper Carlos had brought from Alicia's house was still on the seat where he'd left it. And inside it, Kathleen found the cold, awkward shape of the pistol. If her strength, all that New England toughness she'd promised herself, didn't last as long as it had to, she wanted to have a friend. Her grandfather had taught her to shoot Prince Albert cans in the woods when she was a girl; she'd never shot anything else since.

She looked back at the clearing. Carlos and Juan were no place to be seen. Miranda still sat in the red light of the fire, and the *campesinos* went slowly and steadily about their business of tying their straw windbreaks together. Whole families would sleep out there tonight, she thought. They might sleep that way for weeks. She turned away sharply. Dear God, let them have this land; let her go and leave it to them.

Her eyes adjusted to the thin light of the fully risen piece of a moon by the time she climbed down into the dry wash. It was deeper here than by the marijuana fields, its banks almost up to her shoulders. The cornstalks loomed even higher above her now, like strange, gigantic flowers. Her feet slipped in the sand as she went, and she strained to see far enough ahead of her to avoid the roots that still reached out toward the wash from trees long cut down to make room for more corn. Sometimes she failed, and once she pitched forward into the pebbly sand. For a long moment she lay still, imagining not moving until morning. What if

Juan and Miranda's truck was no longer even there? What would she do then? But a sound behind her—a rock falling from the bank of the wash, an ear of corn dropping—reminded her that soon Carlos would come out of the hut, look for her, maybe come after her. She swung the pistol like a counterweight to help her to her feet, and kept going.

Would Carlos come after her? He could probably have the marijuana fields blazing before she reached town, and so wouldn't need her as a hostage anymore. But she didn't doubt that he'd decided to keep her from leaving at least in part from spite, or hurt, because he thought she'd betrayed him, used him. Would that be working on him strongly enough to make him think it was worth losing the time looking for her?

She slipped and stumbled along the snaking wash for a distance she couldn't measure. She could have gone five hundred yards or could have gone a mile, since her progress was so halting. As she pushed herself to take one step after the other in the maddening sand, she fought the echo of Carlos's voice saying that her true safety might be there with himself and Juan and Miranda. If she simply quit, she wouldn't have to find out if he might be right. But that would mean not finding out about Luis, too. She kept going.

By the time she knew her legs were finally giving out on her, she no longer heard the sounds from the cornfield. Half a dozen times she'd swung the pistol at a noise of things scurrying, crashing, beside her. She remembered stories from Jorge about pumas forced down from the mountains by hunger, bears he had found walking upright from the fields with double armloads of corn. She made coral snakes and rattlesnakes from rivulets of sand in the moonlight. She saw again the pack of coyotes she'd come across beside the river once, tossing a disemboweled cat back and forth among them. She heard wolves in the cawing of crows. And then at last, almost mercifully, she was able only to concentrate on her own labored breathing, her failing legs, the tears that blurred the Venusian shapes of the cornstalks above her.

When she made out the silhouette of the panel truck among the black trunks of the mesquite trees in front of her, she let her legs go, let herself sink down onto her knees as if she were praying.

And even after her vision cleared, she was so absorbed in the pounding of her blood and the clenching pain behind her eyes, that she didn't notice the light beside the truck until she had forced herself to her feet and started toward it again.

It was the steady, even glow of some sort of battery-powered camping light set up at the base of a mesquite a few yards away from the nose of the truck. Had she really been so near to collapse that she hadn't seen it? Or had it just been turned on? She stopped, waited for her eyes to focus better. There was a shape beside it, though she couldn't even tell if it was a man or a woman. Alicia? She felt a stillborn thrill of excitement. No, of course not Alicia. She went down onto her hands and knees and crawled along the wash. The banks were lower here as the wash spread out into a little depression in the flat land, so that she could see and not be seen yet.

She was no more than a few yards from the truck when she was at last sure who she had found. She recognized first the mirrored sunglasses propped up on the man's forelock, then the heavy shape of one of the three men she had seen coming toward her in her country house today. No, she didn't recognize him— she couldn't, not from just one quick look earlier. But she knew what she recognized was a man like those three, and that he had to be one of the men who had raided the *campesinos* she'd just come from. Had he been left behind to pick off strays? Or, more likely, did his presence mean that the other *pistoleros* weren't sure whether Alicia had gotten away either, and were taking the odd chance that she'd have to come to this truck sooner or later?

And if they didn't know where Alicia was, did that mean they didn't know where Luis was, either? She was confused again—in the long walk along the wash she'd almost managed to convince herself that Enrique's men had surely found Luis, that Jorge had even been with them, and that when she got back to Obregón they'd all be waiting for her. Damn this man, she thought! Damn him for ruining that!

And yet he was an ally. If he was Enrique's man—or even a *pistolero* from any other of Jorge's friends—he was her ally. He would have to help her back to town, would have to call her señora and pretend, at least, that he was glad to see her.

But, God, she loathed him. She remembered the

man she'd seen being dragged away from her country house by his hair, the woman with the ragged bandage in the hut, the heaps of ashes and smashed plates and scattered schoolbooks. And he was her ally! She didn't know whether she loathed him more for what he'd done to the *campesinos*, or for what he'd done to the stupid illusion that had kept her going through the endless wash. And yet she had to stand up now, to speak to him as if he were a human being, to ask his help.

As she started to get to her feet, he moved. She waited. He reached down for something beside a rifle leaning against the mesquite, and she saw the red of a Tecate beer can come up into his lap. He got to his feet unsteadily and popped the top of the can, then unzipped his pants. As the stream of urine arched away from him, he tilted the can and drank. The urine trailed away and stopped while he stood, a tottering monument to himself, and tilted the can higher and higher until it was empty. Across the distance between them, she heard him grunt as he flung the can away into a patch of broom. He sat heavily back down underneath the tree, and leaned forward to fumble with the light. In a moment, the light was gone, like a hole in the darkness that had closed up.

The man clearly was drunk. She would have to stand up and go toward him, to call out to him in the darkness. Who would he think she was? Or would he care? Would he jerk himself up out of some drunken half-dream, panic, reach for his rifle? Or maybe even worse, would he realize that she was a woman and in the darkness not care whose wife she was, whose ally he was supposed to be? She sank back down into the wash.

From somewhere in the distance, she heard a low rumbling sound, a sound like a heavy truck or a train laboring toward her up a hill. Yet different somehow, more erratic, and missing the whine of gears or the solidity of steel wheels on a track. She considered rushing wildly toward the highway and flagging a truck down, or following the sound toward a railroad track and leaping onto a freight car. Sweet Lord, was that how far away her mind was from functioning? She dismissed the sound. It was Juan and Miranda's truck she had to concentrate on—how to get past the shape in the darkness and to the truck.

Sooner or later he would sleep. But how much longer would her strength last if she tried to outwait him? And if she made a rush for the truck now, even drunk as he was, he would be on her before she could find the key. That left her the one choice she didn't think she could use. Tentatively, she raised the pistol and propped her hand on the bank of the wash. She could barely distinguish the man's form from the trunk of the mesquite, or from the bushes that were scattered unevenly near it. If only he'd come out into the moonlight!

But she couldn't do it. Not just like that, with no warning, even if he were in a spotlight. Besides, if she missed . . .

The rumbling pushed itself into her attention again, and she realized that it had grown louder more quickly than it ought to have. And now it was clearly no truck or train: there was a kind of hissing to it, a rushing sound she hadn't heard earlier. There was something familiar in it, though she couldn't put any kind of image together. It was hard to tell even where it was coming from. The highway was in front of her, and the Ferrocarriles del Pacifico tracks were beyond the highway. Behind her was nothing but miles of fields, the hut, the wash itself.

Dear Christ. The wash itself. The thunderheads over the mountains at dusk.

She had seen it happen only once, just after she moved to Arizona, before she'd married Jorge. No matter how many times she'd been warned, she hadn't been able to believe in the truth of the warnings then—they had been like stories of Indian ghost dancers or hidden mines to her. Thunderstorms in the mountains too distant for you even to see, and then an hour, two hours later walls of water high as houses rushing down dry washes in the valleys, churning rocks and sand like shrapnel, breaking around bends fast as race cars—old prospectors' tales, she'd thought, stories to frighten the snowbirds away with.

Until the day they had driven somebody's van up a wash at the base of a mountain range, and climbed up to a patch of shade for a picnic. And then watched under a cloudless sky as the van was slammed away down the wash as easily as a matchbook toy in a rain gutter.

Now the sound was loud enough to penetrate the beer-fuddled head of the man under the mesquite.

She saw his bearish shape move as the light broke over the bushes around him again. He held on to the tree and got to his feet, trying to peer beyond the circle of light. Then he cocked his head, listening like a dog, obviously still puzzled but now zeroing in on the direction of the noise. He picked up his rifle from against the mesquite and cautiously made his way through the bushes toward the wash and Kathleen.

She had no sure way to calculate how long it would take the wall to reach her—but the sound was growing more and more rapidly now, turning from a rumble into a loud roar. Minutes, seconds? And the man was weaving his way toward her, was close enough for her to see his ragged sideburns, his tight moustache, his slits of eyes straining to see into the dark. She didn't dare try to make it to the other side of the wash; there was only one direction to go.

She pulled herself up the crumbling bank of the wash. Shouting to him would do no good now: the roar of the water was too loud, too close. He blinked. She was crouched just at the edge of the light, and she would be only motion to him, only a form that he might not identify as human. She saw his unzipped pants and his hands raising the rifle as he must have raised it today at the squatters' camp. Then she focused on his eyes. They were eyes as empty of anything human as if they'd been plucked out by birds. She let her loathing for him, her fear of him, raise the pistol for her.

The first shot missed. His alcohol-slow reaction let him get down only into a half crouch before she

151

managed to grab the wrist of one hand with the other to steady herself and, feeling something half sob, half scream rise in her throat, fire again. She saw him jerk, and the light went spinning away from him. He made it the rest of the way into his crouch, hung there a moment, then sat. He tried to raise the rifle, but it sank.

She was sobbing, running, stumbling toward the truck. Caked mud crumbled from the inside of the bumper as she ran her hand frantically along it, feeling for the metal box with the key, and she felt sharp stones cut into her knees through her jeans. The noise of the water was everywhere now, all around her, and she realized that it was spreading out over the low banks here, reaching for the truck and for her. Her hand touched a sharp edge and she snatched at it. The box pulled away from the metal, but her shaking fingers couldn't hold it; it fell into the blackness under the truck. She swept her hand over the sharp pebbles, feeling for the box. From the corner of her eye she saw the light tumble crazily, then go out. The water was yards away.

At last her hand closed over the box, and in a single motion she was on her feet. She felt a surge of strength, like the first breath after a deep dive. Something clawed at her legs, something full of a dozen hammers. She flung herself over the hood of the truck and let her legs be swept out from under her while the truck rocked as if the ground were splitting open underneath it. There was nothing to grip on the smooth hood, and she felt her knee slam down onto the bumper as her fingers raked across flat metal—raked until they wrapped themselves around what she saw in the half-light was a winged, raring chrome stallion bolted onto the metal for a hood ornament. Crazy gratitude rushed through her for whatever remains of *machismo* in Juan had made him decide to lead his truck along the highway with a winged stallion! Was she sobbing or laughing? She didn't care.

She pulled herself up onto the hood, away from the water that was spreading and losing its force, that she knew would disappear in minutes. She looked along the bank for the man. Where he had been, the water roiled and swirled in the moonlight.

She was aware she was swerving over the road, driving like a drunk herself, trying to keep her vision clear through the endless, heaving sobs. Had a man ever really been there—had she really killed him? Or was that another part of this day, this night, that might or might not really have happened? She prayed that someday she might believe that it hadn't.

Her legs ached from the blows of the rock-freighted water, and her wet jeans clung to her like cold bandages. The heater was on high, but it wasn't helping in the drafty truck. From the radio the *ranchero* music she'd heard at her country house still blared, and her numb fingers couldn't make the controls, whose knobs were missing, work. She let it blare, let it propel her on through the darkness toward—what? It didn't matter; she knew something was rushing toward a climax. Rushing like the flash flood. And she could only ride it now.

The first brightly lit, green Pemex gas station sign at the edge of Obregón seemed to her like something from a space station. Then as streetlights, neon lights, restaurants, sprang up she felt as if she'd been lost for weeks in the desert; they were all as strange to her as letters in a language she'd forgotten. She checked her rear-view mirror, certain she was being followed.

She was surprised when she came to the corner of her own street. Somehow it didn't seem possible that it was still there. It was as if it had no right to be. Families were strolling along the boulevard, making the holiday last as long as they could, and she wondered at them, was almost angry that they dared to do such normal things. She knew that soon the late night drunks would take over the streets, and what hadn't exploded during the demonstrations and parades of the day would surely explode then. How tame that seemed!

Her house was dark, as if nobody lived there: not even the porchlight was lit. The empty house seemed immensely sad to her, like a dead person's coat or dress you find in a closet, that holds some familiar perfume. She drove past as quickly as she could.

She thought it was odd that the police car was gone. Surely tonight of all explosive nights it should be there. Could it have been deliberately taken away, as a signal or a punishment from the government? Or had riots broken out someplace else in town at last, and it was simply needed there? Or was there some other reason, one more unknown thing wrong, one more thing out of place?

She turned the corner by Enrique's house and parked the truck down the street so that an oleander hedge blocked it from the view of anybody at Enrique's— even from somebody in the guard tower. But when she stepped out onto the sidewalk, she saw that hadn't been necessary. The guard tower was empty. When Enrique and Concha were home, the towers were never empty.

No. She couldn't take that, couldn't face another door with nothing behind it. Especially this one, her last possible door. The pain in her legs hobbled her as she tried to run, but she forced herself into a lurching kind of lope, like a woman in a sack race. She was sobbing again by the time she came to the wide, circular steps; and the light from the porch lamp, that one sign of life, drew her limping up the steps.

She rang the doorbell and heard it echo through the house. She waited, rang again, and then to drown out the echo banged on the carved mahogany door until her fist was numb. When she at last heard a lock turn, she realized that her finger was still on the doorbell, that the chimes in the house were still ringing.

The door opened until the latch chain stopped it. Kathleen could only make out part of the face behind it, but that part was enough for her to recognize, with a rush of relief, Enrique's housekeeper. The woman's thin face was fixed somewhere between annoyance and fright. "Señor Enrique," Kathleen blurted. "Where are Señor Enrique and Señora Concha? Let me in. Please. I want to come in!"

The woman looked puzzled, then horrified as she slowly recognized Kathleen. "Señora Zaragoza?" she said tentatively.

Kathleen saw herself as the woman must: hair matted, mud caked, jeans torn, nails broken, and God knew what else. Suddenly she felt as if she were carrying something unclean with her, as if she were wearing everything she'd done this day. "Dear Lord," she begged, "let me in."

The door closed, then opened as the woman slid the night chain off. She stepped back when Kathleen stumbled through the door, as if she were afraid Kathleen might touch her. "Oh, señora! *Qué le pasó?* What happened to you?"

"Is Enrique here? Is my husband here? Or my son?"

"No, just me, señora."

Please, no! "Where is everyone—anyone?"

"The señor and señora went to their country house—they *said* they were going to the country house. But they don't answer their telephone, señora. I'm worried."

"Has my husband been here?"

"No, señora. But he called."

"From Obregón?"

"I think so."

"No—was it from Obregón? Do you *know*?"

"I heard Señor Enrique talking to him, señora—he

was talking about meeting Señor Jorge somewhere, so he had to be in Obregón, no?"

"Meeting him where?"

"I didn't hear that, señora."

"Or when? Did he say when?"

"It was just before they left for the country house, señora. Not long before dark."

"Did they talk about my son?"

"I heard Señor Enrique say his name. Is something wrong with Luis, señora?"

Not long before dark. There would have been no time to have gotten Luis back here—if Enrique had him. And she was with Carlos then, on the way to the squatters' camp, so she could have missed Jorge by minutes—if he had tried to find her. Nothing was clarified.

"Señora, please," the woman said, and Kathleen saw that she was crying. "Sit down, señora. Let me bring you something to drink, please. And a washcloth, señora."

Kathleen couldn't even bring the woman's name to mind; she'd known her for years, and she couldn't even remember her name. No, of course—Inocencia. Inocencia Rosas. Innocence Roses. Yes. Yes, she had to let a woman with a name like that help her. She made her way through the living room, holding on to whatever her hands touched. She was vaguely aware that she brushed something that fell away from her and smashed, but she kept moving toward the kitchen. The perfectly arranged peace of the house nauseated her now, swirled around her like an image

157

in a kaleidoscope. And then she was sitting in a soft chair in a bright kitchen, and Innocence Roses was handing her a glass with something hot in it that smelled of fresh lemon juice and tequila. She didn't remember the woman heating anything, did she? And she heard herself saying yes, making noises of agreement to something the woman was saying while she began wiping her face with the warm cloth. She heard the name Guadalupe and saw the woman was still crying. The hot drink sluiced the dust out of her mouth, opened her throat.

"When did they leave?" she said.

Inocencia stopped, puzzled again. "Who, señora?"

"The police. When did the police leave my house with Guadalupe?"

"Before Señor Jorge called—not long before, I think."

"And has anybody been there since?"

"I didn't see any cars, señora—but I haven't been watching all the time. I know that the two policemen in the car on the corner left when the comandante and those other men who were here did, and I've been afraid. If somebody would kill Guadalupe, and she was the best woman in Obregón, what would they do to me?"

"Left *here*—left the neighborhood, or left this house?"

"This house, señora. Not too long after Señor Enrique and Señora Concha went to the country house."

"Were they here about Guadalupe?"

"They didn't ask me about that, señora. They just wanted to know about Señor Enrique, and the men in the suits seemed to get mad at the comandante when they found out Señor Enrique was gone."

"*What* men in suits? Were they policemen, too?"

"I don't think so. The comandante was very nervous around them, and if he's a comandante, he shouldn't be nervous around other policemen, no?"

The hot drink turned sour now and pushed up against the back of Kathleen's throat. No, a comandante wouldn't be nervous around his detectives, and his detectives wouldn't allow themselves to show anger at him. She remembered the letter from the Game Committee, the formal, businesslike tone, the neat Selectric typing. Men in suits, like businessmen. Oh, God, oh God in heaven. It was true, all of it *true*!

"I want to know about the men, Inocencia. What were they like?"

"*Pues,* like Señor Enrique's friends, señora. There were three of them, a little older than you, I think. Very good suits, nice ties, polished shoes—that's all. They didn't talk much, except to be angry a little, and none of them looked much different from the others. One of them did have hair I liked."

"And did they say they were going to Señor Enrique's country house?"

"No, señora. They didn't say anything about where they were going."

"Then call him again."

"Señor Enrique?"

"Yes, Señor Enrique." Kathleen held her impatience. Inocencia was afraid, too; the tears hung in her eyes, ready to spring.

Inocencia dialed the phone on the kitchen counter. Her eyes darted between Kathleen and the phone. "They won't be there, señora. I've been trying all . . ." she began, and Kathleen could hear the metallic ringing of the phone in the silence of the kitchen. And then in the middle of a ring, a click! "Señor Enrique?" Inocencia said, her voice eager. "Ah! Señor! *Gracias a Dios!*" Her face glowed as she turned to Kathleen.

"Give it to me," Kathleen said as gently as she could, though she wanted to snatch the phone away.

"Señor Enrique? Señora Kathleen is here. She wants to speak to you." She paused a moment, nodded, and handed Kathleen the phone.

"Enrique?"

"Kathleen, where have you been?" Enrique's voice sounded genuinely concerned, genuinely relieved. Kathleen gripped the arm of the chair to keep herself from breaking down and blurting everything that had happened today, letting it pour out in the jumble that it was. "Do you know how many places we've looked for you?"

"Have you got Luis?" she said.

"No, not yet."

She paused, her stomach knotting. "Is Jorge with you?"

"Not now."

"Was it you, Enrique—at least tell me that it was you looking for us today."

"It was me, Kathleen."

"I killed a man. I killed one of your men. He was in the way of the truck, and I had to get back into town. I killed him, Enrique." It was happening, and she was helpless to stop it. She was starting to babble, to break. She gripped the chair arm more tightly.

"Don't tell me about it now," he said, as if she'd started to give him mere details he didn't need. Could he hear in her voice all those things that she felt snapping? "Just listen to me. Jorge is in town. He's gone after Luis. It's going to be all right, Kathleen. Do you hear me? It's going to be all right."

"Jorge knows where Luis is?" Things kept snapping. "He's found him?"

"No, I found him. There's no Game Committee involved in this, Kathleen. It's Alicia Dura, all of it is her. As soon as you left today I sent my people to find out. That's why I came after you—and came after that Dura woman. When we missed you the last time, she contacted me. She'd heard from her people that Jorge was here, and she was looking for him. She said you made a deal with her. Is that right? Did you?"

"Yes."

"She wanted Jorge to confirm it. My God, Kathleen—you offered her everything you've got, to hear her tell it!"

"I did. And more if I'd had it." The tacit criticism in what Enrique said jerked her back from the edge of something, knit what had begun to snap. What damned right did he have to criticize anything she'd done today?

"Well, Jorge's gone to try to talk sense to her. She even said you promised her his money."

Talk sense to her! That's all she thought she'd been doing since she'd first gone to see the woman. "I want Luis, Enrique. Jorge should know that's the only thing that counts."

"We all want that, Kathleen. Calm down and think. How could he get her the money when we didn't know where you were? He went to buy us some time, that's all."

All right. Calm down and think, then. "Why did Jorge come back?"

"He tried to call you, he said. He talked to Guadalupe after you and Luis had left the house and knew something was wrong. So he called me and then got on a plane. He's been going crazy, Kathleen."

"And you told him I had come to you first?"

"He understood. He would have done the same thing I did."

No, Kathleen thought. He wouldn't have—I wouldn't have *let* him, for one thing. "Enrique. Men from the Game Committee were here today. They were here at your house. I'm sure of it."

Was there a pause? Or was Enrique just taking a breath? "I think they were here, too. While I was away with my men, trying to find you and Alicia Dura. My foreman said they were with Aguilar."

"With Aguilar, yes."

"Did you see them? Did you talk to them?"

"No. Inocencia did—and she doesn't know anything. Why would they be looking for you, Enrique? If the

Game Committee's not involved, why are they here at all?''

"They weren't looking for me in the way you think. Aguilar knows that I have more information on what goes on in this valley than he does. If somebody is using the Game Committee's name, they want to find out about it. And Aguilar would come to me first. He always does. There's no more to it than that.''

"You're sure.''

"I'm sure.''

"You knew Aguilar was working for the Game Committee?''

"How do you think I found out the Game Committee wasn't involved in the first place, Kathleen? Look. I don't blame you for having questions. But I'm on your side, remember? If I'm not, and Jorge's not, then who is? Ease up.''

Inocencia handed Kathleen another glass of the good, hot drink. Dear Lord, why was she treating Enrique like an enemy? She was sitting in his kitchen, his housekeeper was serving her his liquor, he'd spent all day trying to help her, he was her only link with Jorge and Luis, and she was cross-examining him!

She put the drink down on the counter without touching it. Whatever she did now, she couldn't afford to lose the precious little clarity she had left.

"I'm sorry. It's been hard today.''

"What kind of shape are you in?''

"I can keep going. For a while, at least.''

"Do you have Jorge's money with you?''

"I can get to it.''

"He might be able to talk Alicia Dura out of the money part of it—I don't know. Do you want to take that chance?"

"No. I don't want to take any kind of chance."

"Then you've got to get it to him, no?"

"At Alicia's?"

"No, God no. She couldn't afford to have him come there. Do you know where the old Casa Blanca club is?"

"Vaguely." She remembered a sprawling adobe-and-tile ruin stretched out under cottonwood trees north of town. She hadn't been there since Jorge had given her his series of grand tours of Obregón when they first married. On that warm spring afternoon, the place had seemed almost romantic to her—the most deluxe of the old casinos and whorehouses that had been Obregón's "boys' town" during the boom days, back before the city had decided to settle into respectability.

"Can you find your way there?"

"I don't think so."

Now there was impatience in Enrique's voice. "A kilometer or so beyond the last Pemex station on the Hermosillo highway. There's a stand of palo verde trees on your right, and just beyond those a turnoff."

"I know them."

"Then you've got it. Go a kilometer or so up the turnoff. How long will you need?"

"Half an hour—I don't know."

"I'll go ahead of you and see that they wait."

"Enrique, no. Alicia's people won't trust you."

"To hell with them."

"No! I can finish this. Jorge and I can."

"I feel bad about turning you down this morning, Kathleen. Let me do this."

"I'm grateful, Enrique. But no, please."

He sighed, hurt. "Will you come back here afterward? We'll figure out what to do next. All of us together."

She knew what to do next. She knew how far the border was, how long it would take to reach it. "All right," she lied.

"Kathleen?"

"Yes."

"Go with God."

In spite of herself, she laughed. "Is he still around?"

Inocencia found her a flashlight and one of Enrique's shirts to replace her ripped one. There were no cowboy shirts in Enrique's closet, only Miami silks, but they would do. Anything would do now, as long as she could only keep moving. Jorge was here, she knew where Luis was—it was almost over, a half hour from being over! The Game Committee was a worry, yes, but now only a back-of-the-mind worry. Their quarrel was with Alicia, and she would get to Alicia before they did. She felt hurt, angry about Alicia—but knew she had no right to be. She had gone to Alicia and begged the woman to let her trust her, hadn't she? Alicia had been playing by her rules all along. Was it her fault that Kathleen was so naive about those rules?

It really didn't matter. In only half an hour, she'd

be done with Alicia Dura and peasant invasions and the whole damned revolution forever.

Her hands trembled with fatigue as she hugged Inocencia in a moment of almost giddy elation at the door, but they would hold a steering wheel, would pull a suitcase from a cave, would help Jorge carry Luis to the truck. It had all been so simple—of course Jorge would come home after he talked to poor Guadalupe, of course Enrique would know to go to Aguilar about the Game Committee, of course Alicia Dura would have written the letter after all!

Her fingers were already fumbling to get the key into the truck ignition before she remembered, and froze.

She hadn't promised Alicia Dura the money. She'd promised it to Carlos, and Alicia had no way of knowing that yet. Alicia *couldn't* have told Enrique about it.

Four

AFEW FAMILIES WERE LINGERING BY FRONT porches, still reluctant to end the day but no longer willing to risk the streets. Kathleen had no choice but to risk them: if she went the back way around the reservoir she'd lose a quarter hour or more in the dark, driving the lumbering, unfamiliar panel truck.

In motion was safety now—safety from her own thoughts and doubts. Alicia could have simply lied to Enrique, hoping to get the money whether it had been promised or not. That was the most reasonable explanation, wasn't it? All the other pieces fell so neatly into place, if only that little one did. She could keep going, she could make it! She shoved the piece a little, let it click into place, forgot it.

Beyond the new motel at the edge of downtown, a city bus blazed. High school kids darted in and out of its light. Some tossed gasoline on it to keep it burning. It was a ritual, a kind of protest she'd never understood. Whenever there was trouble, the first stupid thing student groups did was burn buses. A visible symbol of the government, one they could get to easily? It was another thing about Mexico that was beyond her, that told her she'd never belong here, no matter how much she loved Jorge. She swerved over the curb across the street from the bus to stay as far away as possible from the flames. The police car that came screaming toward the bus ignored her. In her rear-view mirror, she saw riot-helmeted state police, billy clubs flailing, leap from the car before it had come fully to a stop.

Downtown, the sidewalks were still crowded with *campesinos*. Was it that they had no place else to go? Or were they waiting for some sort of signal? She had to slow the truck to avoid eddies of them in the street, and each time she blasted the truck's horn at them, their faces turned to her with cold, passive anger.

And then when the lights went out, there was nothing but flame to light the city.

She was stopped at a traffic light, willing to run it but blocked by the stream of cross traffic, and it was as if someone had simply unplugged the entire city. The blaring *ranchero* music from the radio died and she was sure she could hear a sigh go up, just below the level of real sound, from all the people in the streets and buildings around her.

"They've blown the power station!" she heard somebody yell from the sidewalk, and a cheer rose. Maybe they had, Kathleen thought, shuddering. Or maybe it was only coincidence: you didn't live in Mexico long without expecting the power to go out with maddening regularity. But it didn't matter. What mattered tonight was that the darkness would be an excuse for what had been building for weeks. Behind her she still saw the glow from the burning bus. At one side, a plate-glass window smashed. Ahead of her, with no signals working now, the stream of cross traffic was like a wall. She was trapped. And when would it be her turn, this truck's turn to be burned, dumped on its side, or "liberated"? She reached under the seat where she had left the revolver and laid it on the seat beside her.

Foot by foot she eased the truck through the crowd and into the cross traffic. Cars and people flowed around her, honking and yelling, as long as they could squeeze by. And then it was an inch-by-inch chicken contest with a bus. He was determined to keep going; she was determined not to stop. When their bumpers locked, the crowd cheered again. The bus driver leapt out, fist waving. He had his hand on her door already when he saw the muzzle of the revolver—and Kathleen prayed that it was too dark for him to see how it shook. While he backed away from her, his eyes blinking in surprise, she let the clutch out and edged forward. Metal screeched as the bumper of the bus creased the side of the truck cab, and the crowd cheered again. A hand thrust a bottle of *bacanora* toward the truck window for her. She waved it away.

Sidewalk and street had become one as people took them both over. A string of fireworks went off in the dark and made miniature flashes, like gunbursts. She felt the truck jerk and then saw a man's shape behind her in the truck bed. He yelled a name, and two other men jumped up into the truck bed with him; in minutes she knew somebody would try to get into the cab with her, too, and she'd have lost control, would be part of some insane, tequila-fueled parade. She tried to lock the doors—which had no locks. The only way she could keep anybody out now might be to shoot him.

She kept one hand on the horn, the other on the wheel. She felt soft thumps as the truck shoved bodies out of her way, but she kept going—five miles an hour, at the most seven or eight, but she was moving! Her door jerked open once, just as she bulled her way through another line of cross traffic, and without seeing who was attached to the hand that reached into the truck, she swung the pistol hard against it. She felt knuckles crack and the hand disappeared.

The men in the back of the truck were too busy whooping at the crowd to pay her much attention. But when a parked car in the block ahead went up in a whoosh of flames from a gasoline bomb, one of them plastered a bleary face against the rear window and began slamming at it with his fist and motioning frantically for her to stop. She ignored him, took advantage of the break in the crowd the burning car provided her, and sped up. People were scattering, waiting for the gas tank to catch. Kathleen aimed as close to the car as she could.

She felt a thud as she grazed it, and heard glass break. Somebody screamed at her from a balcony overhead; she risked a glance behind her and saw the men were gone from the truck, scattering with the rest.

She made it as far as the next corner before the car exploded. Her rear window shattered into a spider-web of cracks, and the truck lurched. A traffic cop—the same one who'd tried to confiscate her plates earlier, though looking infinitely more frazzled after two shifts of emergency work—held up his hand for her to stop, then dove for safety. Traffic swerved and braked for him, and Kathleen floored the truck around the corner, off the boulevard, and headed for the backside of the reservoir. . . .

Light from a score of fires pocked the dark skyline behind her as she swerved and careered over the dirt road around the reservoir. Her breath was still coming quick, and now and then she felt a frightening gap in her strength, a moment when her muscles simply let go, when she would try to turn the wheel of the wallowing truck. Twice she crashed through patches of creosote bushes before she could throw her weight into pulling the truck out of a turn. But she felt a kind of light-headed immunity, as if all she'd done today had given her a right to come through this last portion of it intact. And she knew that was dangerous, reckless.

What was behind her in the city worried her less now than what was ahead of her—not just the meeting with Jorge and Alicia Dura, but the other thing she could see in the night sky before her. If there were a score of fires behind her, a whole swath of the horizon ahead of her was in flames. She saw it only as a glow at first, as if the reservoir itself were burning. But as she drove on, trying to keep her attention on the road and to make sense of the glow at the same time, she saw that it was beyond the reservoir, toward the river. And when she realized what it had to be, she knew that recklessness would be her only hope.

There would be no idling into the stand of trees by the river with her lights out, no more than if she'd tried to drive up to a forest fire. For a mile before she reached the burning marijuana fields she smelled the sweetish smoke. And as the truck bounced to a stop, the combination of fumes from the burning gasoline and the smoke made her even more light-headed than before. She rummaged behind the seat and found a bundle of rags, took a large one, and tied a mask for herself. When she got down to the river, she could wet it—and then hope she could get back to the truck out of the clouds of smoke and fumes quickly.

She slid down the riverbank, ignoring the too-slow path, wondering if half the valley were burning like this tonight. She imagined Carlos as an avenging angel, swooping down and destroying, then moving on to create a new lake of fire someplace else. And then she thought, no, it can't be just Carlos, he can't be everywhere. They're all doing it, all the *campesinos* in the valley are out with torches tonight, burning their way to their lands. They're all something from the Book of Revelation, like Mexico itself could be.

She didn't need the flashlight. The fire was reflected from the river in leaping shadows. At the river bottom the smoke was much less, and she took great gulps of air before she dipped the rag in the shallow water and tied it around her face again.

She scanned the bank for any sign of a rifleman like the one who had watched her today. Now and again she saw dark forms move against the orange light, but they were always running, ducking, flinging bundles of flaming sticks to keep the fire going. None stopped to look across the river toward her.

The climb to the little cave was harder than it had been before. There had been time for the aches from her running and falling in the wash to set in, and for the dozen scrapes she had to begin to throb. When she brushed rocks, they felt like knives. The gaps in her strength were more frequent, and when her muscles let go it was as if she had somehow lost her body. More than once she had to give in and lie still against the face of the steep bank until the gears of her body decided to take hold again.

At the cave, she used the flashlight for the first time. The memory of the scorpion was vivid. From where she stood, she couldn't angle the light to see far enough into the cave to spot the suitcase, but the mouth was mercifully clear of the scorpions and rattlers supplied by her her imagination in the half-light. She held her breath and let her fingers crawl toward the place they remembered shoving the suitcase.

They touched pebbles, damp dirt. But no suitcase.

Then it had to have slipped back further into the cave. She hoisted herself higher on the bank, shoved her arm into the cave until her fingers touched bare rock, then raked them across the floor until they scraped against the other wall. Frantic, she scrambled high enough to see, even without the flashlight, that nothing but the flickering light of the burning fields filled the shallow cave.

Her muscles let go, and she made no attempt to stop them. She felt herself sliding down the bank, felt Enrique's shirt ride up on her and catch on her bra, felt sharp stones grating against her stomach. She let herself slide as if she were on a slow sled until her feet settled in sand beneath tepid river water. All she had to do was turn over, roll easily into the water, and float down into the dark reservoir. There would be nothing burning, no red flames above her, no more doors with nothing behind them.

"It took you longer to come for it than I thought," the voice said from behind her, close and calm.

She didn't answer. She didn't know if she could make words form.

"Can you move?"

She tried her muscles, and found that her hand could move. And after that, a whole arm. She tried to roll herself over, but failed. Then a pair of hands was on her shoulders, turning her over, helping her to sit. She almost resented them as they lifted her feet out of the river water.

"Are you hurt anywhere?"

Carlos's face was a foot from hers, his quiet control still in charge, nothing avenging or demonic about it at all. But she remembered the hardness she'd seen behind the quiet before. That was still there, too. "Everywhere," she said, and slipped her mask down.

"I'll see that you get back to town," he said. "Your business with us is done."

"No it's not," she said. "Not until I have my son."

"That's no longer our concern."

She tried to speak, but the words stuck in her throat as surely as the river sand would have. "You bastard," she managed at last. She hit at him, but he stopped her fist as easily as if it had been a leaf.

"If we had your son, you'd get him back," he said. "We didn't break the bargain."

"You do have him," she said. "Alicia has him. You've got the money now, what else can I give you?"

Some of the hardness in his face disappeared. "Señora, Alicia doesn't have your son."

"That's a lie. My husband is with Alicia now."

"Where?"

"At . . . at the old Casa Blanca club outside town."

"Stay here," he said, and got to his feet. She tried to get up to follow him, yet she knew it was useless. By the time she was sure of her balance, he was halfway across the calf-deep water, heading for the other bank.

She turned. She would have to take the path—if she could even make it up *that*. Jorge was at a place called the Casa Blanca club. Luis was there. She would find them, would get away from this nightmare. She was so close this time. She would get there. She would get there.

She stumbled toward the path and began climbing. "Señora Zaragoza," a new voice behind her called, but she kept going. "Señora Zaragoza!"

It couldn't be Alicia Dura's voice. Alicia Dura was with Jorge and Luis at a place called the Casa Blanca club.

"Señora Zaragoza!"

She stopped. Here, higher on the bank, the smoke was heavier. Clarity, she'd told herself. Even through this smoke, clarity. If she started pretending now, lying to herself, she would have been better off letting herself roll into the river, float into the dark of the reservoir. She took hold of the thick red limb of a manzanita bush to steady herself and turned back. "Yes, Señorita Dura."

Alicia was coughing and her eyes were tearing from smoke. She took Kathleen's arm and led her gently back down to the relatively clear air beside the river. Carlos was waiting for them there, and helped Alicia get Kathleen to a rock she could sit on.

"Can you talk to me, Señora Zaragoza?" Alicia said. "Can you tell me what I need to know?"

Kathleen nodded.

"Why am I supposed to be meeting your husband?"

"You wrote that Game Committee letter to my husband," she said mechanically, so weary of lies, of uncertainty, that she willed herself to say it as if it were a fact. "You wanted to meet him to make sure my promise to you was good. You wanted the money I got from our country house. You were going to give Luis back to him."

"Who told you that?"

"Enrique Crouse. He'd talked to my husband. I know he did because his housekeeper heard him. I know he wasn't lying."

"Did *you* talk to your husband?"

"No."

"Where was Enrique Crouse when you talked to him?"

"At his country house."

"And he wanted you to bring the money to your husband and me?"

"But you *have* the money, don't you? How did you get my money?"

"We didn't steal it from you—you need to know that. One of the *pistoleros* guarding this field saw you hide it. He still had it when we took the fields." She gave Kathleen one of her brief, efficient smiles. "You should be grateful for your taste for monogrammed suitcases, señora. We were expecting you."

"Then where's my son? Where's Luis?"

"I've tried to locate you, señora. I went to your house today after our camp was raided, but I couldn't get close to it because of the police cars." She took Kathleen's hand. "The *pistoleros* who raided the camp have your son. I'm sorry, I'm terribly sorry. I tried to stop them, but I couldn't."

"Then why didn't they take you, too?"

"I don't know. They could have. But they only wanted him."

"Do you mean they *let* you go?"

"As best I could tell, yes."

"Why? What possible . . ."

"Señora . . ." Alicia began, then stopped. As she'd done in her house earlier, she gathered herself, considered before she went on. "The only people who would know that are Enrique Crouse and your husband. Again, I'm sorry."

"I know you have him. He's someplace here, isn't he?"

"I swear to you, señora. I don't have your son. And I didn't write that letter."

Kathleen lurched to her feet. "I'm going to find my husband." She didn't know if she believed Enrique Crouse. She didn't know if she believed Alicia. She could only believe what she'd believed before: Jorge was at a place called the Casa Blanca club. He would help her get Luis back. She would find Jorge, and it would be all right, everything would be all right, as Enrique had promised. Her head swam with the smoke and weariness, but she was on her feet. She took a step, then went down on one knee. She pushed Carlos's hand away when he reached for her.

"Señora," he said, with no sarcasm in the word now. "You can't."

"I can." She forced herself up again.

"Where? That club?"

"Yes."

"You can't even drive, for God's sake."

"I will."

He reached for her again, and she feebly batted his hand away. No more fear of him, no more fear of any of them. She started up the path, using her hands, monkey fashion, to pull herself up it. "Alicia," she heard Carlos say, then their voices talking behind her, rapid, too low for her to hear.

And then somehow Alicia was beside her, holding her upright and saying into her ear, "Wait, it's going to be all right," just as Kathleen had told herself a moment before. She relaxed against Alicia's soft breasts and let Alicia pull the rag mask up over her face against the smoke again, efficient but now gentle as a nurse.

And then after a time Carlos's arm took the place of Alicia's, and she felt the hardness of his chest against her as he and she began moving up the path once more. Something he was carrying in his other hand swung against his legs and made him awkward, almost as if he were lame. But everything was spinning around her so much that she couldn't tell what it was.

And at the truck, Carlos helped her in, then climbed into the driver's side, pushing her heavy blue suitcase ahead of him onto the floorboard.

She felt better when they were away from the smoke. Her head was still light, but her thoughts held together in some sort of order now, and the dizziness gradually faded. Carlos was taking the back way around the reservoir, and the jouncing of the rattling truck made talk too difficult to try.

Only when they came to the pavement of the highway—where they turned north toward Hermosillo—did he speak. "Do you still have my pistol?"

She considered lying. But he would probably look for it anyway. "Under the seat." She felt as if she could drink a gallon of water without stopping, to clear the dust and smoke from her throat. "There are two bullets missing."

He nodded.

"I killed a man at your camp." When she'd told that to Enrique, it was like a confession, something horrible she had to unburden herself of. Now it wasn't. Here, with this man, she surprised herself with a feeling of something akin to pride.

"A *pistolero*?"

"Yes."

"Good."

"Is that all?"

"Yes." He glanced over at her. "Should there be more?"

"Yes. There should be more."

"All right. I absolve you." She watched his face for any sign of irony, or that he was making fun of her. There was neither. She felt as if he'd slapped her, drawn her up, reprimanded her. There was no pride possible in that. "Look," he said. "If your husband and Enrique Crouse wanted that money, why didn't they just come get it themselves? They managed to run us away from your country house long enough to do it today."

"Why are you so convinced my husband . . ." She stopped herself. If Enrique had talked to Jorge or if they had arranged to meet, then she knew why Carlos was convinced Jorge was involved. What more could she explain to Carlos? Jorge loved Luis; he wouldn't do anything to hurt him. It was her article of crazy, maybe naive faith—the one that was her last lifeboat now. How could she expect this man to share that, this man who'd left his own daughter for something that was no more than an abstraction, a set of words. She'd feared him, but she knew she could pity him, too. "I don't know why they didn't."

"What do you expect to find at this place?"

"My husband. Waiting for Alicia."

"Do you really expect that?"

She hesitated. "I don't know. Is that why you're going with me—to prove that I'm wrong? That you and Alicia aren't lying to me after all?"

"We don't need to prove that—or anything."

"Then why?"

"I don't know what I expect to find, either. But I'm a savior. People like me save the world, remember?"

"That's glib."

"All right. I could think that all this about your husband and some deserted club is some nonsense you invented. I could believe that you arranged to get your boy back this afternoon, and just now you came to get the money, too. And then you and your husband were going to disappear. But I don't think that."

"Why not?"

"It doesn't fit. If there was a chance to get rid of Alicia at the camp when Crouse's *pistoleros* took your boy, then why didn't they? And what about the letter? If your husband and Crouse could have gotten to the money themselves, why the letter? To have the money and manage to blame the whole thing on us—or on some Game Committee that may or may not even exist? That seems to be wanting to cut *you* out, too, don't forget."

"I won't believe that."

"I know you won't, but I might. Your husband wouldn't be the first man who's wanted to get away from his wife. And if they were trying to blame something on us, that makes me mad. I won't let it happen."

"The Game Committee could still be involved. It *does* exist."

"I've been told God does, too. I've never seen either one of them."

"Some of their people are here in Obregón. They're looking for Alicia—you should be aware of that." What was she trying to do—shock him into admitting he was lying about Alicia? That was what she wanted, wasn't it? She wanted for Alicia to have Luis and for Jorge to be waiting at the Casa Blanca.

Carlos shrugged, dismissing such silliness. "Enrique Crouse told you that, too, I imagine."

It was her turn to nod.

"There's one more thing. I owe you something."

"You don't . . ."

"No, I think you've been doing your damnedest to be honest with us. I didn't want to believe that, but there's simply no way I can make your being part of this whole thing fit. You deserve to get your boy back—if it takes the money in that suitcase to get him, that's why it's here. And if neither of us knows what to expect when we get to this Casa Blanca club, I don't want you walking into it by yourself. Somebody's been trying to screw both of us, so we've both got a stake."

She started to speak, but he cut her off. "And I'm not a damn hero. I'm just mad, remember?"

"All right. I'll remember." She knew she wanted very badly to believe him, to trust him. But if she did, what would she have to believe about Jorge, about her husband? She turned away and watched the light-less countryside take over from the few final houses of the city.

"My last name's Zablodowski," he said. "Would *you* use it if you didn't have to?"

He slowed to let a truck even older and more rickety than theirs pass. The last Pemex station slid by them and was gone. In front of them, their headlamps picked out a solitary stand of palo verde trees. And a little past those, a turnoff.

The moon was high now, already past its zenith. The tall cottonwoods cast short, dark shadows in the moonlight. In open spaces, a pale, almost bluish light robbed everything of color, made it hard to discern the edges of things. Carlos cut the headlamps and crept up the last half mile of rutted road at a pace slower than a walk.

Half a dozen obscure ruins of low, flat buildings spread out in front of them along the remains of a street, and surrounding those, stumps of adobe walls broke the scrub here and there where houses and outbuildings had once been. The only things moving were the tops of the cottonwood trees in the wind. There was nothing romantic about this place; it was desolation, abandonment itself, a movie set for loneliness. Beyond it flat fields swept away toward the outlines of mountains, dark blue in the moonlight, naked, sharp-edged shapes like the spines of prehistoric creatures.

Carlos parked the truck a hundred yards from the first of the ruined buildings, and when the engine died the wind-stirred silence settled over them as cold as the moonlight itself. The popping of the cooling engine was loud as fireworks, and the sound of Kathleen's door closing startled something into a scuttling dash away from a clump of broom beside her. The air smelled of loam and the bittersweet aroma of desert plants at night.

He held up his hand for her to wait. Under cover of one of the stumps of walls, he walked a dozen yards from the truck and set the suitcase down in the shadows. Then he held the pistol up to the moonlight and broke it to see if there was a live shell in the chamber, and motioned for her to follow him.

"I'll go alone," she said when she'd caught up with him. "Please."

"The hell you will." He walked ahead.

As they approached the first building, she saw that the entire entranceway at one time had been covered in shining black tiles but was now gapped with bare spots like sores. Broken neon tubes dangled from a sign over the entranceway: PIGALLE. She shivered partly from the wind, partly from the feeling this place gave her. Its purpose had once been to hold out light against the night, and its darkness was twice as black because of that now. Was this dead place where she had come to find her life again?

Ahead of them in the street, a gust of wind sent a ball of tumbleweed bouncing crazily from building to building, like a drunk begging a last drink. She could see now that long wings extended from all the buildings, wings with rows of torn, flapping screen doors ranged militarily the length of them. Cribs, she guessed, whores' rooms, where the women had brought the ranchers and boom-time *gringos* they picked up in the casinos.

And at the far end of the street, looming two stories above all the other buildings, was the Casa Blanca, the broken man-high letters rising from its roof and silhouetted against the moon-bright sky: C SA BLA/CA. A weak light spilled from its door.

And in front of the door, its hood reflecting the light, a new white Ford sedan waited, like something in a time warp.

"Do you recognize it?" They were too far away yet for a voice to carry to the car, but Carlos whispered nonetheless, as if he were in a graveyard.

"No," she whispered back.

"Could be rented," he said

They kept in the shadows of the buildings as they moved down the street, where Kathleen smelled the mustiness of old adobe from the walls and now and again the lingering reek of urine from doorways. The single light shone from the Casa Blanca club as lonely as foxfire. Inexplicably for such a deserted place, an old newspaper then a beer can scudded past them along the dirt street in the wind, which set up a low moaning at the corners of the buildings and through narrow alleyways as they passed.

And in front of the gutted Farolito Club, Kathleen stifled a scream when they surprised a swaybacked white horse grazing in the weeds of the club's patio. The horse, more afraid than they were, snorted and bounded away into the cottonwood trees. The fright sharpened her senses, so that by the time they were opposite the Casa Blanca, she was certain she could have heard the slightest breath anywhere along the street. But the silence beneath the wind was absolute.

Carlos motioned for her to stay low. Keeping the Ford sedan between himself and the building's front door, he crouched into a run across the relatively bright open space of the street. He stopped beside the Ford and cautiously checked the windows, then waved his hand for her to join him. She tried to crouch and run as he had, but, her heart slamming against her chest, she could only force herself into a slow hobble.

"He's here," she whispered as she pulled up beside Carlos.

"He?"

"Jorge's here, my husband's here."

"Then he's drunk or asleep. He should have heard that truck coming from the minute it left the highway."

"He wouldn't know who we were. He's waiting to see."

"Kathleen. *Some*body's here. That's all you know. Do you think whoever it is couldn't have seen us coming down that street if he'd wanted to?"

"Jorge wouldn't have known who *you* are. How does he know why I'm here, or why you're here instead of Alicia?"

"Enrique Crouse would know who I am. What if he's in there with your husband, Kathleen? *Think*. What do they want?"

"No! I've done enough thinking. I know what *I* want—and what do you want? Why do you want me to slip up on my husband like he's . . . he's something you're hunting?" She stood up. He tried to pull her back down but she shook him off. "I'm too close now, damn you!"

She stumbled backward away from him. He sprang up and grabbed for her again, but she threw herself up a low marble staircase toward the empty doorway of the Casa Blanca. All she had to do was find the light, find Jorge, and it would be over!

"Jorge!" she shouted.

The light was coming from somewhere deeper in the building. She could make out that she was in a wide roofless entrance hall littered with rubble and leaves, and that beyond the hall a room large as a cavern was swallowing the light. She held the wall and pushed forward through the rubble. Just behind her she heard Carlos's voice: "Damn it, Kathleen!"

Struggling, she pulled away from his hands, but he had a grip on her arm. "Jorge!" she shouted again. A moving shadow broke the light in the room ahead of her—there was somebody there! Carlos shoved past her; she saw the pistol raised, saw a glint of light from the barrel.

"Jorge!" she screamed.

The explosion of the shot slammed at her like a fist, violent, physical, and she reeled away from it. Something splattered on her, and Carlos doubled over, seemed to jump backward as if he'd been kicked. Another explosion cut short the echo of the first one, and Carlos twisted toward her. He reached out for her with his free hand, his face in shadow, then plunged toward the wall, glanced off it, and fell heavily into the debris at her feet. She could see his face now in the spill of light from the other room, could see the quiet was gone from it, could see his startled eyes staring up through the missing ceiling at the moonlit sky.

She took a step away from him, toward the doorway to the street. "No!" she said, denying it, willing it not to have happened. Not Jorge—not Jorge in that other room, not Jorge who had done that. She had to get outside, back into the wind, away from the echo of the explosion in her head.

Then she heard her name, and it held her. A voice from the other room, like a rope that held her. "Kathleen." It was firm, a voice she'd never had to be afraid of. And then a form to go with it, cutting a chunk out of the light from the other room. And a hand, reaching out for hers. Enrique's hand, a hand she'd touched a thousand times. She held her own hand out automatically, let him take it and lead her past Carlos's still body and into the cavern of a room.

She blinked in the light, tried to discover where he'd brought her. A Coleman lantern hissed on what had once been a great circular bar, flanked by huge murals of nymphs, Roman warriors, suspension bridges, Watteau picnic scenes, fat nudes, Chinese landscapes. The bar was only a cement form, wrinkled where its tiles had been chiseled away, and the murals were disappearing with their crumbling plaster, but an air of grotesque opulence still hung over the place. Kathleen let Enrique lead her across the tiles of a dance floor to a fireplace large enough to sleep in, where a fire blazed and sent smoke up a rock chimney toward the stars, which she could see through the carved, split beams of the roofless ceiling. Outside a jagged hole in one wall, she made out a patio big as a park with a well and collapsing bandstand in the middle of it, and what seemed to be dozens of the barrackslike doors surrounding it. Arches led off this main room toward other rooms as dark as mine shafts. The impression she had now wasn't of a cavern any longer, but the ruin of some insane, labyrinthine sultan's palace, or a catacomb.

One part of her mind saw it all and registered it. The other part felt only Enrique's hand on hers, leading her toward the fire, and kept seeing only Carlos's surprised face in the entranceway behind her. Her eyes darted around the columned room and looked for a sign that anyone else beside herself and Enrique was in the building. They found nothing but broken plaster, fallen tiles, dead leaves.

"Jorge?" she said. "Jorge's not here, Enrique." Her own voice sounded childlike to her, somebody else's voice. She felt herself floating in a kind of fearful daze, unable to break away from even the gentle pressure of Enrique's hand.

"Come by the fire, Kathleen," Enrique said, his voice soothing and low, the voice she'd heard him use with his horses when something had made one of them skittish. "Your hand's cold."

"I want Jorge. You said Jorge would be here."

"Jorge's not here, Kathleen. I'll take you to him." His glasses reflected the fire, and he looked comfortable, warm, at ease in a wool pullover.

"Where is he?"

"I'll take you to him. He's all right."

"But what about Luis? And the meeting with Alicia Dura—what about all that, Enrique? Why are we here?"

"Luis is fine, Kathleen. You have my word."

"I have *your* . . . how do you know, Enrique? Where's Luis?" She felt her voice coming back, rising and hardening.

Enrique turned to face her, slipped his pistol into his pocket, and took her other hand, too. "Luis is here, Kathleen. You'll see him in a few minutes. I only want you to do something for me first, no? I want you to tell me where the money you brought is, and you can stay here by the fire and warm up while I go and get it. Then we'll go see Luis and I'll take you to Jorge. All right?"

"You wrote the Game Committee letter?"

He hesitated. "I wrote the letter."

"Oh, God, Enrique. Dear, dear God. Why?"

"I'll go get the money, Kathleen, and I can explain everything to you while we're on the way to see Jorge."

She felt it coming back, felt her hardness, the strength she'd known she had when she was bargaining with Alicia Dura in the afternoon. Luis was somewhere near her in these dark buildings. Knowing this sent strength back like a kind of electricity, reaching out for him. "I want to see Luis first. And I want you to take me to Jorge."

"I don't think so."

"You'll have to."

He dropped her hands. "Damn it, Kathleen. Don't you have any idea how much this hurts me?" There was nothing soothing in his voice now. Even his body had tightened and pulled back from her as suddenly as if she'd slashed at him with a knife. Enrique had always been calm, in control of himself and everything around him. She sensed the danger coming from him the way she could have sensed it from an animal, could almost smell it in the air. What had gone on in this man she'd thought she knew to bring her, Luis—all of them—to this day and this place? She had to get to that; instinctively, desperately she understood she had to get to that if she were going to have any chance at all. And she understood, too, that Jorge's survival somehow probably depended on her keeping Enrique from finding that blue suitcase outside in the shadows for as long as she possibly could. Nothing could buy time but that.

"No—I don't have any idea how much this hurts you, Enrique."

"I wouldn't have had it happen this way for the world, Kathleen," Enrique said, his tone again swinging suddenly—this time to a kind of sorrow. "I tried to tell Jorge that at my country house, and I think he realized it was true. *Santos*, we went to school together, and sometimes it seemed to me that we didn't even know whose parents were whose! And I had to face Jorge today, and now I've got to look at you, too, and none of it was supposed to be that way. You weren't supposed to ever have to know, and

193

everything between us could have gone on the way it always had—because I love both of you, and I would miss you the rest of my life. . . ."

Now that the words were loose, they had to keep flowing, to come together into some kind of key. If only she could keep standing, keep her mind focusing long enough to find the key.

He turned and clapped his hands together, then paced away from her. The way the words came tumbling over each other told her they wouldn't stop yet: Enrique was saying what he must have gone over in his mind a hundred times already. "You weren't supposed to get the letter—Jorge was. He would have known just where the money was, and he would have understood about the Game Committee—he wouldn't have gone to Aguilar, so nobody from the Game Committee would have found out. I tried to head it all off, you know—I did! When I sent my men to your country house, all they would have had to do was get there in time to find the money before you took it away, and we could have stopped everything right there. And then that idiot who went to your house to get it—why on God's earth didn't he tell me that he'd been married once to some cousin of your housekeeper's, so that she was likely to recognize him? I could have dressed any one of a dozen others like him up in a suit and sent them, if he'd only told me! I don't know why you shot him tonight, but I swear to you—I thank God you killed the scum."

"You mean the man after the raid. . . ."

He raised his clasped hands and studied them

piously. "I hope at least that helps you, Kathleen, because I liked Guadalupe and nothing was supposed to have happened to her. Or to any of you."

"Yes, it helps me." Rest better, Guadalupe, she thought. I will.

"You see, if you just hadn't found the note, and if Jorge had just come home for the holidays the way I thought he would—he was planning on it, you know, he was going to surprise you—he would have handled it all. And now you're here, and poor Concha's on her way to California and I'll have to spend the rest of my life lying to her about you and Jorge, and I'll have to follow her. But what good will that little bit of money do me then?"

"What would it have done before, Enrique?"

"Everything. I could have kept going here."

"I don't understand. . . ."

"No. And Jorge wouldn't have understood—tonight he said he would have, but before I couldn't bear to think he wouldn't have. He might have even *given* me the money, but what would he have thought of me? Eh? Ever since our fathers died, he told me, 'Enrique, take some money out of the land. Invest it, build with it.' But, no. Enrique Crouse? My family had always had just the land—and I was certain I could hold on to it. Invest? Invest is for shopkeepers and *gringos*, Kathleen. We spent all the money that came in because the land would always be there to bring more. *Verdad?* So when these troubles started building up and the government quit wanting to talk to us anymore, the only place I had to go to protect myself was the land. 'Plant *mota*,' people told me. 'One good crop of marijuana and you're safe. Then let them take the land if they want it, and to hell with them.' So I did, Kathleen. And I took money from the *narcotraficates*, the smugglers who were going to bring the *mota* into the United States.

"Could I have told that to Jorge? Could I have said to him, '*Oye*, *compadre*, I've always bragged to you I could take care of my own land, and now I don't think I can. I can keep the *campesinos* off of it for a while, but I'll never have the chance to harvest my *mota*—I won't have that long. I've been a damn fool, *compadre*. I have to give back a hundred thousand dollars to some gangsters I know, and I have to have some money to live on until I figure out what I'm going to do. Even if this government gives me a little compensation for my land, it will take years."

"We would have lent you the money, Enrique. You know that."

"And when could I have paid it back? Jorge might as well have just given me the money. You should understand, Kathleen. Your husband is Mexican."

Yes, she did understand that much about Mexico. Enrique was *el hombre*, the man. *Campesinos* could ask, could beg. But not *el hombre*. Not *el macho*. He could only take what he needed, however he had to. Enrique was as trapped by this place, by the rules of another kind of game, as she was. And she understood, too, with a sudden, terrible clarity that with every word he was saying, he was digging himself more deeply into his humiliation. It was a humiliation he could never escape as long as he knew that she and Jorge, the witnesses to it, were alive somewhere. It would be stronger than any friendship, stronger even than love. That was her key, and it opened the final door with nothing behind it: Enrique could never leave Mexico knowing she and Jorge were alive.

He turned toward her full on now, and the sorrow had deepened, aged his face. The light from the fire beat against it and made it seem to swim and lose its shape. "It was so *right*, Kathleen. I knew all about your family, no one in Obregón would have thought I needed money . . . if only Jorge had come home when he said he was going to! My life is ruined, too, Kathleen. You know that, don't you?"

"I'm sorry, Enrique."

"For all of us. For all of us. Remember that." He reached for her hand again. The tension seemed to have gone from his body, the way it might have if he'd just made a confession in church. "Tell me where the money is, Kathleen. Give me that one chance."

He could never leave Mexico knowing she and Jorge were alive. "Enrique. Let me *see* Luis first. Please."

"And then the money?"

"And then the money."

He met her eyes, then looked away. "Of course." He tightened his hold on her hand and began to lead her again, this time around the remains of the bar and toward a tall archway that led outside toward the patio and the whores' rooms. A gigantic croupier's painted face grinned emptily at them from over the bar; it was the last thing she saw as she jerked her hand from Enrique's and lunged at the Coleman lantern.

She felt the lantern chimney's heat on her fingertips only for a moment before it slid away from her and over the edge of the bar. It shattered, flared up briefly, and hissed into darkness. She had only a few seconds before Enrique's eyes adjusted to the dark. She couldn't head for the moonlit patio yet. Where had the other arches been, the ones that led off into those mine-dark rooms?

Enrique shouted her name. Already the firelight and moonlight were bringing shape back to things in the room. She dropped to her hands and knees. The knee that had slammed down onto the truck bumper in the flood was as tender as an open wound. A patch of greater darkness stood out from the dark wall a dozen feet from her. She tried to remember the room—there had been an archway closer than that, she was sure. But Enrique would think she took the closest one, wouldn't he? A second lost now might buy her a minute later. Enrique shouted her name again. Scuttling painfully across the rubble from the fallen roof, she made it to the darker patch. Then onto her feet, and into the blackness.

She couldn't even call Luis's name, couldn't shout for him to run, couldn't even let him know she was here! And worse, she couldn't expect him to shout back to tell her where he was.

Enrique had been taking her toward the patio, toward the whores' rooms. Yes, Luis would be there;

each room was a perfect cell, a place where Enrique could have set Luis up with a light to keep him from panicking, and no one could see it. But how could she get to those rooms? Not back through the main bar where Enrique was, and even then, what about the moonlight outside?

She heard Enrique stumbling against something, coming closer. She saw a cigarette lighter flare. He was deciding which archway she'd taken, she knew. Deeper then, deeper into the labyrinth of rooms. She felt her way along the wall until she touched a splintery door, shoved it, felt it give way, and went through it.

A hole in the ceiling filtered enough light through to show her she'd come into some kind of gambling room: cracked cement tables set into the tiles of the floor still had shreds of faded green velvet on them. Roulette tables with depressions in them for the wheel, half-moon blackjack tables—a dozen of them, and another bar. Spiderwebs caught in her hair and she stifled a cry.

Not this room, she couldn't stay here, not with this light. Enrique cursed something just beyond the wall. She ducked behind a table. To her left a stairway led upward into the two- and three-storey parts of the building—toward what?—private gambling rooms, wrecked offices, more stairways that might lead out only into the empty air now? No, she had to stay down here, near Luis, near the open refuge of the fields beyond this building.

To her right was a door in the corner of the room—

and no other direction to go but back. She crawled on her hands and knees, keeping the tables between herself and the doorway Enrique would come through, reached the door, pulled the handle down, shoved. . . .

It didn't move. She drove her shoulder into it; it rattled and the dry wood creaked, but it didn't move. She couldn't hold back the sob that came now as she pulled herself upright by the door handle, then threw her whole weight into it.

It gave, opened an inch. Something heavy was blocking it. She shoved again, heard something topple, and the door rasped open a foot more. And that was enough. She squeezed sideways through it, feeling Enrique's silk shirt rip, feeling her breast scrape against the rough jamb.

She was outside now, in the patio—outside while Enrique was still somewhere in the darkness behind her! She pushed the door shut again, and tumbled the piece of roof cornice against it that had been blocking it before. She lost more seconds in piling three other heavy pieces of cement on top of the cornice. If Enrique tried the door and couldn't make it open, would he think she'd taken the stairs? That chance was worth the seconds she lost.

The whores' rooms stretched out on either side of her. Which way now—left, right? Lord Jesus, she'd need a quarter of an hour to check all of those rooms. Something caught her eye, just a half dozen rooms down the wing to her left. Was it light seeping from beneath one of the doors? Enrique shouted her name again from inside the building, muffled, but closer.

And then again, and she could tell his voice was coming from somewhere above her this time. He'd taken the stairway! She headed for the light.

The screen came off in her hand and clattered onto the tiles, a noise that could be heard for a mile, she knew. And when the other door opened, the moonlight rushed into the empty room, glinted even more brightly off the broken glass that had tricked her. She backed away from the windowless room. There was only a gaping, vacant saint's niche in the wall to show it had ever been inhabited.

Frantically, she flung open three more doors. No. Stop, damn it, she told herself. Think, *think*. She let her eyes leap from door to door down the length of this wing. Surely some light would seep out around these cracked and dry doors! But there was none, not even the false reflection of the moonlight.

He'd stuffed the door with newspapers, with rags—that was it. Or, God forbid, he'd lied again. Luis wasn't here after all. . . .

She hobbled toward the other wing, her eyes running along it from door to door ahead of her. And when she saw the faint line beneath one of them she almost denied it, almost went on. She checked her elation, made sure that it didn't take hold this time, even though the line of light seemed even and much yellower than the reflection of the stark moonlight.

But then as she got closer, she was sure. It was light! This time she opened the door gently, almost hesitantly, afraid—afraid of not finding Luis, afraid of finding him.

He sat on a camp stool against the back wall, a candle stub guttering on a piece of broken roof tile beside him. When he saw her he wiggled down from the camp stool, started toward her with his arms out. Then he stopped and his eyes turned resentful, angry. She'd abandoned him, he was saying. Where had she been? "Go away," he signed to her, and the wonderful, terrible childish absurdity of that made her feel as if her chest would explode.

She bent over, not caring about pain now, and wrapped her arms around him. He struggled briefly without real enthusiasm. Then she felt his tears on her cheek and heard those sobs without words that had been his only way to tell her of his grief for so long.

She lifted him, and he wrapped his legs around her waist and buried his head in her hair. Across the patio, she thought. She'd have to risk the moonlight— find a gate and get into the fields as quickly as she could. Once she was there they would be hidden, safe, and in the morning there would be *campesinos* in the fields. And Enrique wouldn't risk harming Jorge as long as he knew she was still alive.

The flare of the lighter was bright as a spotlight when Enrique flicked it a yard away from her eyes. She turned her face to the side and closed her eyes against it. "Noooo," she said. "God, noooo."

The light vanished, then she felt his hand close around her arm, not rough, but firm. He knew she couldn't run with Luis in her arms, that she wouldn't fight the pistol he held in his other hand.

"What did you gain, Kathleen?" he said sadly. "I

told you, the money and then you're all right, you're free.''

"Enrique, please," she said. "You're his godfather. He trusts you, Enrique." She smelled Luis's child-smell, felt his knees against her ribs, and pulled him even more tightly against her.

Enrique was leading her again, back toward the huge room with the fire. "He's right to trust me, Kathleen. Only you think I want to hurt you. Haven't I kept Luis safe for you? Didn't I get him back for you? Now he and I will go get the money together, and you'll wait for us here. And when we come back with the money . . ."

As they stepped through the wall-high archway into the room, it exploded with light. Three sharp, white beams of light that seemed to burn at them from the crumbling murals themselves. Enrique tried to pull back into the patio, but a beam of light drilled at him from there, too. And as he pulled back, he let her go—let her go to throw herself forward toward the lights. She didn't care where they were coming from, who was behind them, just that the light meant there were *people* here!

"Señora, stop please," a voice said from behind one of the blurred circles of light. It was a man's voice, and it hadn't asked her to stop, it had ordered her to. She strained to see behind the lights, which seemed to be powerful hunting lights, trained now exclusively on Enrique. But she could see nothing except the hands that held the lights, the sleeves of business suits above the hands, and indistinct bulks beyond those.

"Señor Crouse," the same voice said, metallic and echoing in the empty room. "The Sixteenth of September Game Committee accuses you of falsifying documents in an attempt to damage the good reputation of the Committee. It is the consensus of these assembled representatives of the Committee that you have attempted to unfairly manipulate the Game in violation of long-standing rules and customs which were clearly known to you. That is a very grave offense, Señor Crouse, with specific penalties prescribed. Have you any evidence to offer to the contrary?"

Enrique swung the pistol toward the voice. Almost as if there had been a signal, all the lights tilted upward toward his face, blinding him. He began to speak, coughed, and began again. His voice seemed swallowed by the room. "Talk to your man Aguilar. He knows who wrote the letter."

The second voice, the one she recognized as Aguilar's, came from a dark space between two of the lights. "We have been listening to your telephone, Señor Crouse. And we have been here listening since you arrived."

Enrique feinted as if he were going to try to rush the patio. The lights shifted slightly with him, then he ducked and broke for the archway Kathleen had hidden in earlier.

She brought her hand up swiftly to hold Luis's head down against her shoulder to keep him from seeing, and closed her eyes. The collective sound of the guns might have been loud enough to penetrate even his silence, or he could have only felt the concussion. But he twitched in her arms until they stopped, until only the terrified flapping of the wings of fleeing birds was left of sound.

When she opened her eyes, she saw in the hard lights that Enrique had made it almost to the door of the gaming room. Now he lay as Carlos did, looking up.

The lights flicked out, all but one, which trained itself on the tall archway to the patio. The metallic voice that had spoken before said, more softly now, "Comandante?"

"It will be cleaned away by dawn," Aguilar answered from the darkness.

"*Bueno*. Señora Zaragoza?"

"Yes." The steadiness of her own voice surprised her.

"My apologies that we aren't able to offer you transportation back to Obregón. I would imagine, however, that Comandante Aguilar could arrange . . ."

"I don't want to go back to Obregón. I want to go to my husband."

"The Committee's business is done, señora. I'm not authorized to speak to that problem."

"Do you know where your husband is?" Aguilar asked.

"Enrique said he'd talked to him tonight at his country house. You heard him."

"There was no mention of your husband's presence in any of Señor Crouse's telephone conversations from his country house, señora."

"That doesn't mean anything. Go there with me."

"If you'd care to come back into Obregón with me, I'll be happy to send someone out to . . ."

"*No!* Now!"

His tone turned final, official. "Señora Zaragoza, I advise you as strongly as I can not to go to *la familia* Crouse's lands tonight—I *forbid* you to go, for your own safety. Señor Crouse's . . . employees will be very nervous, as I'm sure you understand. You have your own transportation and are free to return to Obregón in it, or to accompany me. At daylight, you have my word that I will send someone out to Señor Crouse's lands—something I will have to do in any case."

He was forbidding her to go to Jorge, when Jorge might still be in danger. Who knew what instructions Enrique might have left with his men? Or if it might not be too late even while they stood here in this mad . . .

Luis moved against her. His body was loosening, relaxing. She knew he would be asleep soon. *She* could go to Enrique's, but what about Luis—and what if something had already happened to Jorge? Who would be left for Luis then?

And she'd thought it was over! Luis's weight seemed to increase as he relaxed, second by second seemed to become too much for her to keep holding up. "No," she said to the place where Aguilar's voice came from in the darkness. "I'll get back to Obregón by myself."

"So you understand me, señora? You may not go to Enrique Crouse's lands."

"I understand you."

"Then *buenas noches*, señora. I'm pleased that this hasn't turned out worse for you than it might have." There was a moment of silence. "We are at your service."

Kathleen didn't answer. He was telling her that she should be grateful to him for his being here, for the fact that only Carlos and Guadalupe and Enrique Crouse were dead so far. Let him rot, she thought, in whatever part of hell "official" things like him went to rot!

The light moved toward the archway, then paused. The metallic voice behind it said, "You will be gratified to know that the Committee has decided that you and your family will be exempt from participation in the Game, señora, should your name ever be drawn in the future. Your money is yours to keep, of course. It is the Committee's gesture of goodwill."

She turned away from the light. Goodwill! In the entranceway she stopped beside Carlos's body. Luis was breathing in the heavy, even rhythm of sleep now, and she couldn't put him down. She stood by the body, listening until the footsteps in the patio had died away, until she heard a gate open, then the sound of a motor starting in the fields behind the Casa Blanca. The dying fire popped in the next room. The sound of birds' wings and the cooing of doves told her that the club was being repopulated. She hoped dawn would come soon, that Aguilar's men would arrive before the vultures she was sure were beginning even now to tighten their slow circles above the club. She leaned against the wall to ease Luis's weight and let her silent tears well and flow until there were no more left to come.

No. She couldn't take Luis to Enrique's country house. No. She couldn't abandon Jorge there. What was there to do then but stand here in this ruin beside this dead man who had tried to help her and grieve for him? For him, for Guadalupe, for poor Concha somewhere in California now, all of them. For all of us, she thought.

She knew it was almost dawn; the subtle change in the cold light in the entranceway—not a brightening really, only a change in tone—announced it. She shifted her weight and pulled away from the wall.

In the street, the change in light was even more noticeable. The obscure shapes that the buildings had been last night were hardening, gaining lines and edges. She knew that soon the bleakness of the dawn here would be overwhelming and that she couldn't stay.

By the time she'd reached the end of the street she could make out the panel truck clearly, and the piece of a wall where Carlos had hidden the money. She laid Luis down gently on the seat so that he wouldn't wake, then brought the suitcase and slid it into the cab on the floorboard beside him. Morning birds were cracking open the silence of the night; in

Obregón delivery trucks would be out. She rounded the cab to the driver's side, limping still. The sun's red light would break over the mountains soon.

The two rooster tails of dust caught her eye just as she was about to get in. The light was still too dim for her to be sure that she saw them at first, but as they drew closer, she could tell that they were coming along the road from the highway—along the road toward this place. For a moment she considered running from them, starting the truck and driving as far into the fields as it would take her before it mired or lost itself in a wash. But what was there to run from? Enrique's *pistoleros* were dogs without a master now and would be thinking of their next jobs as soon as they saw his body. Aguilar's *federales* would do their work and leave her in peace if she asked them to. The Game Committee had faded back into its anonymity. She leaned against the fender of the truck and waited.

The first car that came into sight she recognized as the old Valiant she'd seen parked in front of Alicia Dura's house when she'd first gone to see her. The second, hanging back out of the Valiant's dust, was her own Ford.

"Oh, dear God," she said under her breath, and pushed away from the fender. She started toward the cars to meet them, trying to run, trying to shorten the distance, to make them reach her even the smallest fraction of a minute sooner.

The Ford slid to a stop in a cloud of dust that caught the morning light like smoke. It rose and billowed around Jorge as he stepped out of the car, then started toward her.

To pull a counterraid on Enrique's country house had been Alicia's idea, Miranda explained to Kathleen as Juan and two other men took Carlos's body from the Casa Blanca. Her anger at the raids by Enrique's *pistoleros* had been boiling in her all day, and the news Kathleen had brought her about Enrique's blaming her for the Game Committee letter had pushed the pressure higher than she would bear. Burning the marijuana had helped, Miranda said, but Alicia wanted to do more than that—she wanted to stop the raids for good. And the only way to do it was to fight back, put the *pistoleros* on notice. That they had found Jorge at Enrique's house hadn't surprised Alicia much, Miranda said. That they had found him in a store-room with a man holding a rifle on him had; she'd been more than ready to convince herself that he and Enrique were partners.

Alicia let Miranda prattle, and didn't contradict her. She was more concerned with Carlos. The *federales* wouldn't get to bury him; she was determined to see to that, she said, and so they had to get him away before the *federales* showed up. Kathleen wondered if deaths like this had gotten any easier for Alicia over the years—her father, Carlos, and how many others? Or had her grief only learned to be more private? In any case, she was as efficient as ever as she saw to the business of getting him in Juan's truck to take him back to Obregón.

Luis slept until Jorge eased him into the back seat of the Ford. Then he opened his eyes and saw Jorge in a half dream, Kathleen was sure, and smiled just before his eyes closed again.

No one had mentioned the money in the panel truck, as if by a silent, common agreement. Alicia finally went to the truck cab, got in, and when, after a time, she climbed out she brought the suitcase with her. She brushed Juan away when he tried to help her carry it, and set it firmly down by the trunk of the Ford. Her eyes were red from the smoke, and she moved slowly and heavily.

"This wasn't part of our bargain," she said—to Kathleen, not Jorge.

"It would have been," Kathleen said.

"But it wasn't." She gave Kathleen and Jorge together one of her brief, businesslike smiles. "I kept a commission. The king's fifth. We need seeds—then there's damage to Juan's truck, belongings to replace for the people at your country house . . . and a down payment on your farm equipment, Señor Zaragoza. I'll take your word that we can work something out for the rest."

Jorge answered Alicia's brief smile. "Why not? You'd wind up with it all anyway, eventually."

Alicia considered. "True. But we may need your help one day, no? After all, now that we have the land, somebody's got to teach my people something about managing it. We'll have better luck with you if you know we owe you money."

Jorge's smile returned—a smile Kathleen realized how much she'd missed—and he opened the trunk to put the suitcase in. "As a leftist, Señora Dura," he said, "you make a damn good businesswoman."

"I'd better be. We can't have the revolution going out of business." She took Kathleen's arm. "Walk me to my car," she said.

Kathleen knew that the dawn and Jorge's coming had given her her dozenth—and surely last—wind. But for now her mind still had some edge left. The softness of the Ford's seat and the sleep that she prayed would come could wait a minute more, though not much more. She followed Alicia.

Alicia nodded toward the north. "Headed that way, I imagine."

"Yes."

"For good?"

Kathleen hesitated. "In a way."

Alicia raised an eyebrow. "You've lost me."

"I'm not Mexican."

"I had noticed."

"But I've been trying to be Mexican all along—for Jorge's sake. For his family's and his friends'. I found out today—yesterday—that it hasn't worked."

Alicia waited for her to go on, noncommittal.

"The problem is, I don't know where home is anymore. I'm not Mexican, and I walk around carrying more of Vermont with me than I ever thought before today—but Vermont's not home, either."

Alicia put her hand on the door of her Valiant. "*Bueno.* I'll tell you one thing you are. You're a good woman. For what you've done this past day, I respect you. We both made some rules for ourselves,

212

no? Maybe that's enough to do or to be for now. Go north for a while and let it all settle, get the taste out of your mouth. Mexico will still be here—different, I hope, but still here. Eh?'' She took her hand off the car door and gestured toward Jorge, who was leaning into the back seat of the Ford to cover Luis with a blanket. "You love that man? You think he's a good man?"

"Yes."

"Then he'll help you figure out what you are. You'll work it out. A little Mexican, a little *gringa*—that's not such a bad combination. Just remember this: you don't have to *be* Mexican or *gringa* or Venezuelan or anything first. You just have to be somebody you can live with.'' She opened her car door and smiled again. "Just look at *me*.'' She got into the car, which made a slow, unhappy sound as she started it. *"Adiós,"* she said, and touched Kathleen's hand.

"Adiós.'' Kathleen took a step back as the car clanked and pulled away. She watched it bounce its way onto the ruts of the road, as she shaded her eyes against the new, naked sun that Alicia was heading toward. When she looked away, she saw that Jorge had finished spreading the blanket over Luis, and was standing beside his door, waiting for her. She turned away from the growing sun, threw her shoulders back as best she could, and walked toward him. Walked New England tough, Mexican tough, knowing that whatever came, she could find her way home.

The
Best Modern Fiction
from
BALLANTINE